A VERSION OF ME

Askew's
Word on the Lake
Anthology
2024

Fiction, Nonfiction,
and Poetry from
Contest Winners
and
Presenters

Word
on the Lake
Writers' Festival

SAW
SHUSWAP
association of
WRITERS

Table of Contents

From the **Shuswap Association of Writers**

On behalf of the Shuswap Association of Writers, I would like to thank all the contestants who entered this year's Askew's Word on the Lake Writing Contest.

This is the eleventh year that we have offered the contest, to encourage, promote, and reward writers not just from our local area but from across Canada.

A special thank you goes to our judges, who gave generously of their time to adjudicate the many entries in three categories: nonfiction, poetry, and fiction.

We would also like to thank Askew's Foods, who became the sole sponsor of the contest at its creation eleven years ago, and who have continued to support the contest ever since.

This year, we also wish to thank Simon Fraser University and the Writer's Studio at SFU once again for their donation of three online creative writing courses for the first-place winners in each category.

I must also thank Mary-Lou McCausland and Virginia McCausland for starting the writing contest and the *Word on the Lake Anthology*, and Scott Fitzgerald Gray for his work the last five years to make the contest a continued success, and for expanding the anthology in both print and e-book formats.

This year, the Word on the Lake planning committee are looking forward to presenting our anniversary festival in Salmon Arm, at the Prestige Harbourfront Resort and the Salmon Arm Campus of Okanagan College.

We have a full slate of dynamic presenters and entertainers lined up and look forward to a fun celebratory weekend.

Best regards,

Kay Johnston
Shuswap Association of Writers

Since its inception, Askew's has sponsored the Word on the Lake Writer's Festival. This festival encourages new, emerging, and seasoned writers to celebrate the full diversity of the word and the gifted writers who guide us in our exploration through their stories and poetry.

Listening to storytelling, writing, or reading a book builds bridges to a world of fellow readers. Askew's believes our sponsorship of this writer's festival provides value to our over-all community by supporting our creative community, which contributes to the health of all with the sharing of creativity and knowledge. The sharing of creativity can then produce goodwill by establishing a sense of connection with the listening, read-ing, and writing audience.

Askew's ongoing presence in the community for the past ninety-five years has given us the opportunity to help sup-port Salmon Arm's rich population of writers and storytellers through sponsorship of this festival, which we are proud to support.

David Askew,
President and CEO,
Askew's Foods

I am I: and I must follow that furrow, not copy another. That is the only justification for my writing, living.

— Virginia Woolf

For the **Forest**

Sherry Cassells

They say the best time to plant a tree is twenty years ago. Same goes for telling the truth. Best time would have been right after Tom died; I mean, what's another blow when the pain's already more than you can take?

We called my grandfather's acreage a *farm* at first, although it was nothing like the neat green rows with scattered cows and bubblegum pigs we expected. I couldn't get a grip on the size of the place, though — acreage is difficult to quantify. It's like measuring peppers in pecks, and when I asked him to explain, my grandfather said, *Acreage is a state of mind.*

He called the farm a tree conservatory, which was the main reason my father made fun of it, and when it was revealed to my brother Tommy there would be no *moo moo* here and no *oink oink* there, he didn't take it well.

Fuck's a tree conservatory? my driving father said, the stripes on his shirt fraying into the sky above our new convertible, my mother beneath a triangle of silk and perfume, her lipsticked mouth laughing as she turned to Tommy. *There there, Tom, he's still got Minky,* but the old dog was no consolation and Tommy continued to mourn.

I thought the idea of a tree conservatory divine.

•

This morning, I crash through the milestones going back.

It's been twenty years but change is gentle in the country-side, unlike the view from my condo where the skyline tumbles in perpetual flux, allowing new buildings with strange shapes — there's one like a sail, and when it overlaps the moon I feel an unmooring. But here on the road, time has nowhere to display its progression save the trees, their differences and also their similarities, and then into view hurtles the octopus oak I used to watch for, adorned with running shoes, each pair tied and flung over its boughs.

Tommy asked *Why,* his curiosity rode him, filled him, and he demanded *Why why why.*

I had an ability to count, was always and still am a counter, and it looked to me like an entire grade's worth of sneakers: 59 pairs, 118 singles.

My mother finally said, *That's where somebody died, Tom.*

Tommy was easily broken. As sensitive people go, he was at the very quick, and the truth he pried out of our mother, that it must have been a young person who died, ruined him for the weekend.

Until that tree, I don't think Tom knew that young people died.

Twenty years have turned the shoes grey. It's as if the tree is now bedraggled with Spanish moss, as if its branches have been hanged.

Next, the tin house always catching the sun. There's an increase in sooty blackness at its edges and it seems heavier, as if the hay fields wild around it are digesting it, the hollow farm-houses further deteriorated, the three bridges also heavier. The locks at the Severn have been modernized, fishermen in boats bobbing here and there on the water while their black trucks wait on the shore like so many beetles. The cottages bordering the weedy lake have not been overtaken as my striped father predicted — *Poor suckers, those joints'll be swallowed up in no time* — and in Tommy's eyes I had seen it happen.

I am going back, crashing through, getting there. My window is open, the stripes on my shirt consider departure, I chain-smoke invisible cigarettes.

All along like clouds on the horizon, the trees bubble, my quantifying mind goes on count again, and I reel in the ever-accumulating sum. Tommy could count without counting too, but about the trees, he'd say, *There's only one, you know, they are all together*, and I'd look at him, catch his melting smile.

I remember how me and Tom hooted, exhilarated, when my grandfather showed us a sphere of dirt in the palm of his hand and said it contained more life forms than there were people on earth. The enormity of it thrilled us; the numbers in our heads jostled and spilled in a kind of euphoria.

I knew right away when Tom started using. I was not in his vicinity but I knew like roots know, I knew he was shooting up. I phoned him and said, *What are you on?* and he said, *Heroin mostly.* His confidence soared, his sensitivity was replaced with chunks of abandon, he yelled, *It's like I am mainlining words, I can talk to anybody*, which certainly appeared to be the case. For when I got home winded and alarmed, there he was at the kitchen table talking to our father who sat silently in his pyjamas, flannel stripes dark and firm. The minute I walked, in my father walked out as if through a revolving door.

Tom said, *Try some,* and I did through my nose, and right away we up and left, barely fitting through the door. We were many angled and splattered with inspiration, we counted the stars and were up all night until shredded, we sifted through the door at dawn and to our beds, eerie and suspicious. For the doubts, absent for so many hours, returned uncountable, and I knew Tom's were exponentially heftier.

I have never been able to assemble my grandfather into a form. I cannot picture him; I know his hands were like my own, I remember the colour of his eyes, I'm told I walk like him. The problem is that in my mind, he lives as a ghostly mosaic containing only the atmospheres of his conservatory — what ekes from dirt, the back and forth of oxygen and carbon dioxide, hurtling molecules, space, the fizz above Lake Superior over which pines loomed precariously, their upright brethren pulling for them he said, saving them, providing nourishment.

When we were young and subject to bedtime stories within the dark gnarled world of fairy tales, I used to look over at Tom and take his hand under the blankets when necessary. My mother read the words as if she were dictating a distant weather report, our drunken father like Marlon Brando; he bowed to the tale's kings and fought its enemies, scorned the heroines for their weakness one night and their strength the next.

Our grandfather's house was smack in the forest where nothing is quiet ever, where slices of sunlight arrived scented with the breath of the whispering trees. I have tried to build his image from these visceral sections of light too. It has become a sort of hobby, there are sparking moments in which he flashes like the hologram I saw at Burning Man the summer Tommy died.

I always wonder the moment, for surely there was a beginning, when the terrain of Tom's mind began to distort. And then I have to wonder in another realm of possibility harder to touch, was it ever smooth to begin with?

On my grandfather's land was a shoreline where the trees broke to allow rock. It was the edge of the Canadian Shield, the portion of continental crust underlying the majority of North

America, and there was something about its cool largeness I loved. I needed only count to one, and this rock dove into Lake Superior, another gigantic one.

The lake was named not because it's the best of the Great Lakes, but because of the French words for its position: *lac supérieur*, which simply means *upper lake*. The rock itself, the shield, ekes out pines along its edges — imposing beasts who dig their heels into scant earth. Relentlessly shoved by the wind, their disfigurement is permanent and exquisite.

When I swam, I felt I was up for digestion.

My grandfather remembered where each log used in the construction of his house had grown, and he pointed over their billowing brethren in the forest, saying to me and Tom, his disciples, *There's the beech, there's the ash, there's the balsam, the poplar, the maple, oak oak oak, hemlock, the birch.* Contrary to architectural norms and scientific laws, he used all varieties of trees that grew in his forest; he felled them by hand, and positioned his logs vertically.

Nothing again will ever make me feel as safe as I felt within the walls of that house — my superfluous father, my simple mother, my savant grandfather, my brother Tom with whom I felt in a way conjoined, and my skinny young self whose job it was to protect everyone.

Within those walls, I was off-duty.

When I think of heaven now, it's not the usual paradise. It is the square interior of my grandfather's house plunked in the forest of my childhood.

•

Three hours jonesing for the forest.
I kiss my fingers, fake-smoking.

Field rock cow field rock cow, like Fred Flintstone running through his house — table chair window table chair window, field rock cow field rock cow.

When walking through a forest, look up, my grandfather said, and he continued to float words by us like objects — root network, soil fungi, light dependency. We learned to trust our feet, especially Tommy who went ahead of me, his small feet flitting over the terrain swiftly and accurately while I stubbed and stumbled behind. *Look up, look up*, my grandfather yelled at me while he marvelled at my brother's fluency, Tom's ears reddening with his praise, and the next day Tom tried barefoot, his white feet strange in the forest like ghosts.

Now I think the forest, in those fluid barefooted moments, made Tom their own, and he never again found peace anywhere else.

On the way home, he hollered to stop the car, and when my father finally pulled over we were right at the octopus oak and Tommy ran out. My parents started arguing, he pissed, and then hurled his shoes up the tree and got away with it, his beautifully successful first act of defiance.

There is never a moment of truth, never a moment of revelation. There is only acceptance.

We went to the conservatory almost every weekend of our childhood. When I woke in the night, Tom sometimes wasn't in the bed beside me; I looked into the square room's corners where he often curled, but it was through the window I saw his feet like white rabbits among the trees. I lay back down. I can't tell you how frightened I was both *for* and *of* this moon-lit stranger who came back to bed and found me crying, said, *There there*, his cool hand reaching across the gap for mine.

It is a rare thing for me to lose count, but by the time my grandfather died, I'd lost count of Tommy's defiances. Our parents put the conservatory up for sale, which alarmed me until Tommy told me it would never sell, that he'd had a word with the broker.

I have since purchased the acreage, which is indeed a state of mind.

Tommy never tried to hide his drug use from me; he never tried to hide anything from me. We spent much of our time together even as our lives spread apart, and once a season, we went together to the forest, through the teeming landscape, beneath our father's faded stripes and the same pastel galaxies I drive beneath now, the road smaller smaller smaller closer closer here.

My grandfather's house surrounded by his forest, his conservatory, where — had I told the truth — I would have put Tommy's ashes, not *scattered* them, but *put* them in the seams between earth and root. I would have pressed them into bark, packed them between needles, made a paste from them and painted leaves with their stucco, dappled some onto my own tongue.

Now for the truth: Tommy didn't die like I said. His body is not lost in Lake Superior. There was no heroic struggle unless his struggle with life itself was heroic. He died in the trees, and I cut him down, planted him, and lied about it.

In the forest, there are unwritten guidelines for etiquette.

First Place — Fiction

What an absolute delight to read this story. From the very first line, "For the Forest" is a masterclass in voice and poetic prose. The structure is also very interesting, with the circularity of the acreage used to frame a tragic biography of the narrator's brother. Very well executed!

— David Brown

Invisible

Kristine Laco

We wore plastic lanyards with Unaccompanied Minor in large letters across the front. Inside mine was my boarding pass with a red carbon back and a note from Dad in his neat square printing, giving our mother permission to pick us up at the Toronto airport. My heart fluttered, anticipating our reunion and the excitement she promised to uncover: the CN Tower, the Royal Ontario Museum, the Science Centre. Her world was so foreign and mysterious, only two hours away.

Beside me, my younger brother Mark opened the ashtrays, pulled at the little table, and fiddled with the chair back. His blond hair was never in place. I combed mine, but didn't wear my mousy hair up or in braids because Dad didn't know how to teach me. Schoolyard mothers would offer to help, but I always said no.

"Wanna play Hangman?" Mark asked. He used his lanyard as a noose, popping his tongue out and tilting his head.

"Stop that," I said, swatting his hand before I added, "Sure, I'll play."

We tore the plastic off the gifts Dad had given us for the flight and shoved the garbage in the seat flap. We held invisible ink pens between our pointer and middle fingers. The orange cap and white barrel reminded us of the cigarettes mom used to smoke when she lived in Thunder Bay, and we mimed puffing and dropping ash in the little tray.

I removed the cap with a pop, then found a Hangman puzzle in my book.

"Time starts…" I paused. "Now!"

We raced to complete our phrases while the plane loaded. Filling in the little circles for the letters, revealing the clues.

"Have you flown before?" A woman in a uniform interrupted us.

"No," I answered for both of us. "This is our first time."

"Why are you going to Toronto?" she asked, smiling.

"Our mom lives there," Mark said.

The woman's smile was intact, but she held her head to the left and her eyebrows drew together. I'd seen that look of confusion on others.

"So you live there?" she asked.

Mark replied without looking at her. "We live in Thunder Bay with our dad."

Women asked me about our home situation. They asked me where my mom was when I was getting my hair cut, when I was getting fitted for dance costumes, or why Dad brought me shopping for underwear. Their voices increased octaves when they'd reply directly to Dad. I hadn't thought it was different for Mark. I always whispered my motherless shame or shrugged. Mark answered as if it didn't matter.

He continued with Hangman. The woman moved across the row. I saw her bend at the waist and tilt her head towards us. I heard the words "mother" and "alone." My face flushed. I wrung my lanyard between my hands and turned to the window.

People with orange vests waved signals. They blurred, and before I could blink off the tears, a shiver rolled from my shoulders to my spine.

Mark tapped my arm. I brought my sleeve to my face, then turned around to see his concern.

"I'm afraid of the flight," I lied.

I fingered Dad's note. What if our mom didn't recognize us, forgot to meet us, or if we got lost trying to find her? It had only been six months since she moved away from her life and her family. I didn't know how long it took to forget.

"Hey," Mark said. "Let's play another game." He puffed his pen and flicked the end, then returned to the book.

"Nah," I said.

Instead of playing, I watched the action through the window. Home fading. White cotton sky filled the distance between us and Dad. As the clouds broke and a big city came into view, I wondered if she had watched through this window when she left us and was blinded by the same sun. Had she uncovered some secret and sighed, safely distanced while she flicked her ash?

"Tray table up," the woman said.

Two bumps to landing. We slowed and stopped as my heart rate quickened.

"Done," Mark said. He closed his book, now on his lap.

I still had puzzles to solve. I was not done.

Honourable Mention — Nonfiction

Adventures, no matter how great or small, constantly put things into perspective and show us what's truly important and what isn't. While we tend to focus on grand adventures and what we can learn about humanity in general, it is often micro-adventures — especially at a young age, and in the company of one's sibling — that show us life is more about experiences and connecting with loved ones than a collection of possessions. "Invisible" not only tells the story of two unaccompanied minors on a flight to Toronto, but tells how we can support each other with just the simplest of gestures. Something we all need reminding of as we make our way along the winding road of life.

— Chris Brauer

Retraced **Storefront**

David G. Brown

She hesitates at the veggie shop. Got some lovely tomatoes —
that's a close translation; he adds extra Rs like loverly and
termayters. No eggs today, or eggs'll be in tomorrow, and those
apples are deee-lish, and every jingle he's said a hundred and
thousand times, and he says them again and again and steps
outside to light another smoke. But beyond one houseplant, she
can't remember shopping here before, not for vegetables, probably, but, somehow, the old man's mannerisms seem familiar,
maybe once or twice they do, but not regularly, she'd not have
come here often, not on a post high school income or with
anything approaching a codified value system, like cheapest
is best, and even though we've returned to that philosophy by
circular means, she'll still commit to buying a few things from
the veggie stand, a yam and head of lettuce, and yes those eggs
are actually cheap, so certainly the eggs. And isn't that a nice
investment in posterity, or history, or something she can't quite
name but it seems more wholesome than the proper market up
the street.

She used to live here, she tells the veggie man, just up there
on Rockland, got my first houseplant from you she says, that's
right, and what a relief for them both, these cornerstones of

industry and patronage, hearkened to community or some such extinct institution, and what a relief, to have someone to talk to, both again, even in this passing oblivion. And yes the year's getting late, the root crops are all up though there's never a shortage of taters, is there, and we can still get strawberries in winter, somehow, yes, we can have anything at any time, and bicycles rattle by and the riders have little speakers tucked in ears and they're laughing at a joke from another continent, and as much as we love these things we suspect them for their excesses. They both agree on this point.

And just up there, just three blocks away, she used to go to the beach with Douglas and the black lab, and they'd try to get down miles of shoreline by only standing on the logs and mounds of driftwood, cuz touching the ground was insta-death, acid or lava or worse, and they acted twelve years old more than twenty, even when the subtext was a surprise pregnancy and his funny not funny accusations of theft at work, and what all that shit led to in the end. It was always that way with Douglas. You looked at him and just knew that was a short and bright fire, and you made what you could with the time you had.

These coffee shops are as steadfast as the chestnut trees, she thinks — the chain and the local, squared off and still in deadlock, years later, though the bakery is gone and the restaurants have all changed names, and once she waffled here too, like we've all dated baristas from time to time, but she started at the convenience store, eighty cents for a large and those hazelnut creamers were prime on an undeveloped palate. And then to the chain to learn what real coffee was, maybe, and now, present tense again, she's talking to some new boy, another wannabe internationalist, or that's what his profile says, and he could be her Internet goldfish, and if all goes well she might end up in his spiderweb, so now she calls him the text-message boyfriend, and that's a step closer to real life, and he says let's go for coffee in the village, maybe, and okay sure, and yeah sounds good, right, and he asks which cafe do you prefer, and the option raises too many questions like who is testing whom, but this interview and application process will continue, so of course, yes, what else but the local. Let's meet at the local, she says, with the braids and beards and scarves and thick black glasses. Yet the option could have meant any number of things and nothing.

And all around them the great chestnuts are more like war elephants than horses, plodding down the street, keeping pace, with the massive trunks straddling the cars slipping through in miniature. Yet the entire procession is invisible to the jumbled crowd gripping tables and mugs beneath patio heaters at the mocha house, the modular hominids swilling fears of robotics acquisitions and synthetic intelligence, and this yin against the potential of tidal power and decriminalization and bluegrass night at Orange Hall. When you come back here, you think it's so pretty it's gross, these massive Victorian mansions all carved up into permaculture suites, heritage yes indeed, or otherwise we'd just call them apartments or flats or studios. But she still appreciates it like she did on that first visit, a million years ago and more.

So there she is in line, acquiescing to the proper market, queued to trade plastic paper for foodstuffs, to complete the quarter-circle rotation, waiting for the shuffle of divider bars, waiting for the shift of eye contact and the autonomic exchange, listening to conversations left and right, and the theme is unchanged and eternal. Time is a river, they say, or a carousel. Like prices going up, grapes a dollar thirty when they were always a dollar, or last month if never, and chocolate kisses aren't what they used to be, are they, don't you remember when they were good as anything, and it's all turned to rubbish, it's all rubbish but the morning sun's steaming off the clouds and there's blue coming in at the cracks and you can smell the sea from here.

The smell of the trees and beach for miles and Douglas always talked about the smell. Nothing like Salmon Arm or Cow Town or anywhere probably. That faint sulphuric undertone at the shore, the heaps of bull kelp, the piles of blanched wood, all sticks and roots and trunks washed to silver. Even up on the mountain that wasn't really a mountain, they'd walk around the base and the longest way, the lab in and out of every tree must have covered ten times their distance, the day they smoked a joint in the mine shaft and then got scared they had used up all the oxygen and crawled out in a dumb panic. Especially up there you had to think how clean the air was, and Douglas always would, this island like a bio-dome or a wildlife preserve, he said, though most everyone seemed quite tame in the end, even when he'd been locked up for assault. But at twenty-two, that was still childhood. And they'd climb up the steep sandy path all the way on the other side, three quarters the way round. They'd climb up into the sunlight, up above a temperate canopy of cedar and maple and fir, and they'd stare out at green and sea and ignore the angular betrayals of human habitation, and she'd say hey Douglas, did that guy get back to you yet, and two seconds later the pager chirped in his back pocket, and Douglas would say holy shit are you psychic, and she'd laugh and shake her head because the prescience seemed to go in both directions.

Up the street and again between the coffee shops, and this is where the new strangers meet and will meet once more, maybe, the veteran girl and the goldfish boy, the new one, this is where the talk walk begins, a loop to the water and back through the park, how romantic, sussing reciprocally, like where do you see yourself in a year, and do you want kids, or do you still want kids, and let me tell you about my most life-changing moments. But we'll leave out past relationships, of course, that's taboo as sex talk at this stage, and it feels more like a work meeting than a date, and then that wind is quite cold so probably we're both thinking about putting on more clothes, undressing hardly, and when he texts afterward we begin to see the process and trepidation that moves in all directions, like you seem fun and not crazy, thanks for the walk, though you were hard to read, not sure, but I'd like to talk more, if you wanted to go on a hike or what.

And so she leads her goldfish to the mountain but never once mentions Douglas. They take the same route, east around the base, three-quarters round, then up the steep side, sit in the sun and have a beer, but just one since she drove, and now the pager is a phone, and a moderately intelligent one, and the goldfish falls behind and sneaks a text, nodding like he's still listening, and when the path widens she walks beside him, close enough for their arms to touch but he moves away, ahead or behind, locked in a bubble, and sometimes body language is all we have because the rules of speech are fast and probably ancient. With each meeting she gives up and checks out, but then his es em es innuendo is all ex ex ex and oh, his fast forward alter ego, so yes they have dinner, her place, just up the road, and she fucks up the chicken, maybe a bit, but the potatoes and salad are rad, yet he cuddles up into the furthest corner of the love seat when they watch a movie, something smart and funny she says, and he rests his feet upon the wide stool with room enough for both of them, but when she puts her feet up too he takes his down and pretzels like a Zen master. She wiggles and becomes further entangled and maybe when they hug goodbye she finally feels him alive and scared and scarred and human, too.

So a day and a week and up the street and homeward, she gets another carton of cheap eggs, would never mention the two that were bad in the last dozen, returns her used carton, and veggie man says thanks dear and that's great and he loves it when people bring their cartons back, and today she's buying eggplant and tomatoes and fresh basil and he even notices the difference and comments, and she smiles and doesn't really know if she should but she smiles and says she's cooking dinner for a boy, for a scared goldfish, two strikes third pitch, like once, at least, that meant something reasonable, but the neighbourhood's changed so much and your heart starts to hesitate at even the smallest expectation.

In **St. Mary's** Parish

Lindsay Curry

The sinners have all left for the night.
The girls, too, have long gone home. They go
by names like Crystal, Lola, Scarlett, Destiny,
and Angel, but when not dancing, they are called
Sally, Roberta, Tammy, Charlotte, and Patrice.
Now, there's only me and Father Francis.

Priests aren't supposed to frequent strip clubs,
but he says he's here to pray for the souls
of the girls. Who am I to say he's not? He prays
over their bodies — studies them, to know his flock.
I tell him, you should be praying for the ones here
to watch. They're the ones with a choice, after all.

"Time to shut 'er down." He gathers up his overcoat
and hat and puts his left palm on my right shoulder.
"Go in peace, Monique." His right hand moves
through the air in the sign of the cross, blessing me
even though I run this unholy den.
Or, perhaps, because.

He trudges to the door as I wish him good night —
or rather, good morning. Three and a half hours
till Mass; I say I'll see him soon. Time enough
for a shower to wash away the profane
before I present myself in the house of the Lord.
I finish counting the night's receipts, smooth

out a crumpled twenty: my contribution to today's
collection. The janitor comes in the back door, ready
to mop up the unmentionable. He lifts his hand
in a wave, silent as always as he readies the club
for another day. I down one last shot of tequila
and find my way Home.

Second Place — Poetry

*The juxtaposition and layered perspective of this poem took me
out of the ordinary into the extraordinary.*
— Sheri-D Wilson

For **King** and **Conscience**

Juliet Hill

They were kind to him at the Metropole. That was something. There was a quiet acceptance among his colleagues at the theatre; a shared understanding that people didn't always respond well to too much questioning. Four years of war and an epidemic had worn away and sensitized the skin of those who'd survived, and there were plenty like him in the town. Perhaps some thought he was a little odd or reticent, but they didn't press further.

If anyone had asked him about the limp, he'd have given them the lie he'd prepared when he first became William. There was shrapnel embedded in his leg, which had come from a daisy-cutter exploding a few yards away from the trench he was sheltering in. He practiced describing what happened, made sure it was consistent, and had even tried it out in a public house before he came home. Now he almost believed it. None of his family remained in the Yorkshire mill town, and there were few who even remembered his parents. Sometimes people looked at him closely and asked if he was one of Frank's sons, but nobody ever asked if he was the soldier or the conchie. The limp did the trick.

When he was still Claude, he would smile at strangers. Now he never did. His job in the theatre box office meant he was less visible, hidden in the dark behind a metal grill, and he covered his abruptness with a studied professionalism. When Kitty suddenly appeared at the window that day, he knew that she wasn't sure it was him, and he quickly turned away before asking a colleague to deal with her question.

But when she came again a few days later with another obviously invented question, he knew he'd have to show himself.

"I thought it was you the other day, but it's so dark in there I couldn't see, and then you disappeared. How do you bear so little light?"

"It's not so bad. You get used to it."

He remembered writing that exact phrase in a letter to his parents when he was first sent north and billeted with the other objectors at the military prison in Richmond Castle. He'd thought they might be worried, but their concern for his well-being was outweighed by a shame so all-encompassing that they left the town to start again elsewhere. From that moment, Claude knew that they would speak of only one son, William the soldier.

He took Kitty to a tea shop opposite the theatre, where he could see the posters for yet another Gilbert and Sullivan opera being plastered on the red brick.

"Did you recognize me, Claude? The first time I came to the window?"

"Of course I did, but I'm William now. I didn't want you saying my name."

"I would have been discreet, you know that. I don't tell people I worked with conchies. I just say I was a nurse, nothing more. Anyway, I never thought you'd do it, pretend to be William, I mean. I thought it was just talk."

"It was talk. We were all joshing and I said that if William was killed, I'd pretend to be him, given that my parents would prefer him to survive. I never thought he would die. I can't believe I was so stupid and insensitive, to joke about something like that."

He didn't want to admit to her that he'd enjoyed saying it, that he'd hated William ever since he had joined up and taunted Claude for not doing the same.

"It's different now. I have to work; you know it's impossible as a conchie."

But she was still thinking about Richmond.

"Who was that man who would cry if anyone mentioned Whitby?"

"Ralph."

"That's it, Ralph."

She took a sip of coffee.

"Then there was Douglas."

Dougie. Nobody believed much of what he said, but they indulged his stories of stage success in London or poetry reading tours in America. They even sat through his interminable readings of Medieval Scots poetry, which everybody knew he'd written himself.

Kitty was the only staff member who let her impatience show, and given that she reported directly to the prison superintendent, Claude knew how vulnerable it had made Dougie feel.

"He wasn't so bad."

But Kitty wouldn't let it go.

"Douglas-Campbell-from-the-Highlands with the booming voice, who'd once performed for King Edward." She shook her head. "It was so unnecessary. Especially when we all knew he was from Nuneaton.

At first, Claude laughed a little. It was the first time he'd laughed in a long time, and it felt good. But then he remembered Dougie's nightmares and what he'd told him about his past. Still speaking with the put-on accent, still calling him laddie, so that Claude was never sure who Dougie had been or what had really happened to him. They'd all been hiding something.

"Have you seen Archie?"

He'd wondered how long it would take her.

"No."

"He was quite ill with the influenza."

He said nothing in the hope she'd move on, and signalled for the waitress to bring the bill. The last thing he wanted was to start thinking again about Archie.

But she persisted.

"He's living in York. I saw him a few weeks ago."

He couldn't help himself.

"You saw him?"

"He asked if I'd seen you, and of course I hadn't then. He's been looking for you, but neither of us realized that you were William now."

She paused as if deciding how much to say, and then it all came out at once.

"Can I tell him I've seen you here? I never understood why you didn't want to keep in contact with him. I'm not blaming you, honestly. I know you were in a bad way too, but he was very upset. I know he really wants to see you, to try and … I don't know, make things better. The two of you were so close."

Could she ever really understand? To have said what he said to Archie, foolishly thinking it might be reciprocated. Then having to live side by side with him, with Archie now knowing that Claude's studied indifference and sexual sophistication had been false. He just wanted to forget.

They sat in awkward silence as the waitress cleared away their cups. Then Kitty stood up to leave and handed him a piece of paper.

"He had some very bad news." She looked directly at him. "His friend died from his injuries. You know, his friend on the front."

She couldn't have made it clearer.

After she'd gone, Claude recalled one of the first conversations he'd had with Archie. Sixteen hard-line objectors had been taken to France to be court-martialled and nobody knew if there would be more. Archie had said something about wanting to go with them, but when Claude, assuming he wasn't serious, made a joke about it, he didn't laugh.

"My friend is in France. I'd like to be closer to him, in case something happens to one of us."

Claude knew by then what he meant by "friend," but he still didn't understand.

"Surely it's better to stay here and stay alive. It's not as if you'd be able to see him in France if you were a prisoner."

But Archie just shrugged.

"We quarrelled before he left, and I don't know if my letters are reaching him."

Months later, Claude understood that irrationality all too well, and often wished he could go back and change his logical but thoughtless comment. But it probably wouldn't have helped Archie and his agonizing wait for a letter — a letter that in all likelihood remained in the superintendent's drawer.

Sometimes Archie spoke more openly about their relationship.

"James thinks we'll never be fully respected if we insist on being different. That's why he joined up. He reckons the country will realize the debt it owes to people like us when the war's over."

He shook his head.

"Why should we have had to join their war in order to be treated like human beings? The government want to humiliate us into fighting, but we should direct it back at them. As Marx said, the government should hide its face in shame, not the people. If our kind of bravery, what we've done here, isn't acknowledged, there's no dishonour in that for us, only for them."

Claude often had a feeling that Archie was rehearsing his arguments for the next time he saw James, and he couldn't help but resent his lesser status.

From the day of Kitty's visit, it took Claude more than three months to take a train to York and visit the address she had given him. He'd gone back to work that afternoon with no intention of doing so, but he couldn't bring himself to throw away the piece of paper. By the time he did, he couldn't forget the address.

The woman who answered the door of the grubby-looking boarding house looked him up and down as if she invariably had low expectations of anyone who knocked.

"Archie Carr? Would you be a friend of his?"

"A long time ago. Not exactly a friend, more of a work colleague. We worked together for a while. Does he still live here?"

"No, he's been gone this last month."

Claude wasn't sure if he felt disappointment or relief.

"He was arrested, and I haven't had word since."

"Arrested?"

She looked at him hopefully. "He still owes me three shillings."

Claude nodded and gestured for her to continue.

"One of my neighbours said he'd got hard labour. How she knew, I don't know. She said he were caught in some sort of police raid, indecency she said, but I'm not one to gossip."

Claude paid her quickly and left.

When he walked past the theatre on the way home from the station, they were once more plastering posters onto the wall: The Metropole Varieties with *Douglas Campbell's Caledonian Coronach* topping the bill. He smiled. So Dougie was still performing, and why shouldn't he? He'd always been more comfortable behind a mask; maybe they all had. Only Archie had the courage to be himself.

At work a few days later, one of his colleagues started whistling *The Conchie's Lament* under his breath just as a smartly dressed young man appeared at the window. Claude said nothing until he'd left.

"How do you know?"

"What?"

"That he was a conchie. How did you know?"

His colleague shrugged.

"He's the type. Come on Will, you know. A pansy boy."

There was something in his tone that stirred a long-buried memory, though Claude was unable to grasp it before it evaporated.

He stood up and looked directly at his colleague. Nobody spoke. He thought of Dougie and his spectacular ability to re-invent himself after a life of abuse; he thought of Kitty with her good intentions but instinctive distancing from an unpopular position; Archie and his refusal to conform to a predetermined role. His herringbone jacket pushed against his chest and he struggled to breathe.

"My brother William was killed at the front. My name is Claude, and I spent the war in Richmond Castle as a Conscientious Objector."

Nothing about being a pansy. That would have to wait many years.

They had been kind to him at the theatre until then. When he left and moved to another town, he wasn't missed. But at least he was Claude.

Second Place — Fiction

"For King and Conscience" showcases a profound emotional turning point for a young man who decides to own the truth of his identity and his past. Strong imagery and dialogue work in concert with a crescendo of tension.

— David Brown

The Cat at **Dunbeg Fort**

Chris Brauer

(From *Lost Between the Stones and the Sea: A Journey of Discovery in Ireland.*)

During tourist season, the nearby visitors' centre features audio-visual displays, a craft room, a small cafe, and a seafood restaurant. Since it was not tourist season, mine was the only car and everything was closed. I did, however, find a bit of company. The resident cat — orange with a snow-white chest and feet — was lying on her back, basking in the late-afternoon sun, where picnic benches are set out during the warmer months. She seemed content, in the absence of noise, so I sat down quietly on the brickwork next to her.

Her eyes smouldered with a quiet intensity. The golden hues burned like hot coals that could reignite the bonfires of Beltane at any given moment. And yet there was a hint of playfulness — of mischief managed, of forbidden adventures, of secret pleasures. The suggestion that not everything is as it appears to be.

I warmed my fingers in her fur before she sat up, and together we looked out at the wild Atlantic and watched the dark grey clouds envelope the land and sea. The islands were no longer clear on the horizon, but a blur beyond the tumbling of the tide. What had been delicate muslin folds above us was now the weight of slow, dirty tears. There was no longer the roar of wind or of water. The world fell into an immortal silence.

We walked across the road and I paid the man sitting in his shack a couple euros, which seemed to be the going rate to trek across someone's field and have a look at ruins. With the cat beside me, down the slope we went and along a pathway fenced on either side. We followed a narrow stream that runs parallel to a low stone wall and, though the sun was no longer visible, the waters reflected a dreamy glimmer as it cut into the earth.

The ground seemed to heave and swell as the ancient structures came into view and I had to stop a moment to centre myself. As we arrived at the outer defensive banks, it felt as if we were momentarily leaving behind one world and entering another.

Though Paula and I had walked through the rampart passageway years earlier, as the early people would have done, it was now no longer possible. This section of the fort has since been wrapped in fencing and closed off to the public after much of the western wall fell into the sea due to storm damage. The Office of Public Works and National Monuments Service sent personnel to investigate damage to the site shortly after the storm, but there was nothing they could do to prevent more from eventually falling away. One day, the entire structure may fall into oblivion and future generations will have to rely on photographs.

Within the earthen banks, I could spy the sea through the linteled doorway and thought back on those that took part in the building of this ancient site — placing and balancing stone upon stone to create a solid defensive structure without mortar of any kind. Wondered how difficult it was to maintain hope in this unforgiving landscape. It would have taken enormous courage and fortitude to make a home thirty metres above the unyielding and unrelenting waves that crash against the black rocks.

After following the fencing, I managed to find a way in and discovered the ruins of the *clochán* (dry-stone hut) at the centre of the site. The interior of the wall slopes, forming steps, presumably to give access to a parapet or for seating during communal events. Plunked myself down and the cat sat at my side as I tried to imagine what daily life was like at Dunbeg — what sounds competed with the constant roar of the sea and howl of the wind. Was the crackle of the fire and the sharpening of bronze and iron with circular stones a soundtrack for the women who wove or dyed cloth with cold, cracked hands? What stories did they as tell as darkness fell? What lullabies did they sing to their children? Did they look out towards the open ocean and wonder what lay beyond? Did they feel a presence guiding them during quieter moments of reflection?

Together, the cat and I mused on the passing of time — the ceaseless transition of season to season, but also the long history that turns all to dust. "Then shall the dust return to the earth as it was," I whispered, "and the spirit shall return unto God who gave it."

The cat looked up at me, and we made eye contact before both turning again to the churning waters. The Celts considered cats to be guardians of the Otherworld and keepers of ancient secrets. I half-expected my furry friend to clear her throat before engaging in metaphysical debate. But she didn't say anything. Instead, by giving me permission to sit with her, I was gifted with the knowledge of continual present — with no sense of the temporal distinctions of past, present, and future. "It feels as if nothing exists but right now," I said to the cat. "All memories and worries are nothing but illusions."

Tears of peaceful contentment rolled down my cheeks as we continued to look out towards the unrivalled beauty that can only be found at the stark edge of creation. "There is a stillness here," I continued. "And maybe, in that stillness, a little bit of magic that allows one to get in touch with the sacred experience of life."

The cat stood up in response, and then yawned, stretched her back, and sauntered around the wall. She waited for me to follow and, as it is no use arguing with a cat, I stood up and rubbed the cold from my legs. Instead of walking with me, she took the lead and I followed behind.

We were about halfway up the hill, when she turned around, sat down, and gazed out towards the promontory. The cat looked up at me as I approached.

"I believe it was Polonius…" she began.

"Pardon me?"

"Polonius… who told Hamlet, 'To thine own self be true.' "

"Ah, right."

"It begs the question, then: How often do you feel you can truly be yourself?"

"Is this something that's been on your mind lately?" I asked.

"Not really. Just the last little while."

"Oh, I see."

"Philosophers throughout history have held the idea of authenticity in high esteem. There is our *outer* authenticity — how well what we say and do matches what is really going on inside us — and our *inner* authenticity. This refers to how well we actually know ourselves, and are aware of our inner states."

"Why are you telling me this?" I asked.

"I'm getting there," she said. "Have patience."

"Sorry. Go on."

"No one is fully authentic all of the time in their outer presentation. Sometimes we need to put on an act to get by. But some people spend more time living inauthentically than others."

"Do you think that is *my* problem? That I'm not living authentically?"

"I think that there is a part of you that feels you must now rush off to town because you need to somehow justify being out here. Despite all that you have learned, there is still a level of resistance. There is still a little voice inside you that stirs doubt in your heart. But you need to tell yourself that it's okay to spend your days walking up mountains alone or wandering through archaeological sites with strange animals. You don't have to feel embarrassed or ashamed that you need more of that in your life than the alternative. I know that you want to push yourself outside your comfort zone, and make conversation in crowded pubs, but that is not the reason you came here — even if you think it is. The reason you came here — to the edge of the world — is to listen, observe, and reflect. You came here to understand that you are connected to everything and everyone by golden threads, even if sometimes you don't feel it. You came to find solace in all that you can see with your eyes, and all that you can feel with your soul. And then you will go home, pour yourself a thimble of decent whiskey, and write."

"I've been trying," I said.

"Yes… well… in the words of one legendary Jedi master, 'Do. Or do not. There is no try.' "

"Mmm," I said. "Very good."

"Anyway, as I was saying… if you ever feel trapped — in your job, or in a relationship, or in the culture in which you are living — and rarely get the chance to be yourself, then you damage the true essence of who you are. More damaging, however, is when you don't know yourself and it is your inner authenticity that is compromised."

"I appreciate your concern," I said, "and your words of wisdom. But I'm not rushing. Though I may not always feel connected to the place I call home, I *do* feel a connection to *this* place — and maybe that's enough for now. Even if I'm not able to return for many years, I now understand the connection I have to the natural elements: the eternal battling of light and shadow across land and sea and sky. To all the stories of the stones, carved by those that lived and loved so long ago. To that which exists just beyond the borders of this world, where time moves in mysterious ways. And maybe, by spending a few more days here in Ireland, I will confirm who I am and how to best follow my inner authenticity."

"Hope so," said the cat. "Remember that conformity is a form of cowardice. Don't feel you have to be something that you're not. Remember what Alan Watts once wrote: 'Waking up to who you are requires letting go of who you imagine yourself to be.'"

"I will," I replied. "Promise."

There was suddenly a sharp noise behind us. I turned around, looked down the path and out towards the never-ending blanket of grey. I couldn't locate the source, but there was now a subtle hint of blue on the far horizon. The patchwork of farmland once again became a verdant applause.

When I turned back, my feline companion was gone. Figured she had either concluded our conversation and slipped off in search of adventure, or had merely continued up the hill.

A few minutes later, after crossing the road, there she was — lying on the brickwork, where we first met. I sat down next to her and, after warming my fingers in her fur, she looked up at me. But she didn't say anything further.

It was time to take my leave. I was getting hungry, and was looking forward to a couple pints, so I patted her head one last time and whispered a thank you. Stood up, rubbed my eyes, and took a couple deep breaths as I looked out at the setting sun. In a haze, I buckled myself into the rental car and drove off.

It was only when nearing town that I began to doubt what had happened. I could neither confirm nor deny that I had spent time with the *cait sidhe* (the fairy cat). What had earlier seemed so clear was now beginning to fade away, like the last remnants of morning fog. Had our strange conversation actually happened, or had I imagined the entire thing?

Perhaps, I concluded while crossing the stone bridge on the edge of town, it doesn't matter. Perhaps, like so many other aspects of Ireland, it doesn't need to be explained. Doesn't need to make sense. It just needs to be felt.

Beyond **Time's Reach**

Matthew Heneghan

"Time heals all wounds?" It's a perfectly wonderful turn of phrase. A conjecture steeped in positivity and idealism. It is, however, in my estimation, a fallacy. A gentle lie fabled to ease the burden of pain felt by those left behind. Time is something that simply passes irrespective of our involvement. It's not *time* that heals, it's our will. There resides an inconvenient truth in this world — and it is that to manage one's pain, one must endure it. It is the only way to conjure the strength needed to find a way to tomorrow. Time does not lessen pain so that it becomes more tolerable; it grants the opportunity to build the strength needed to carry it with us for the rest of our corporeal days.

This may seem overly bleak, or even a little macabre. I promise it's the opposite. I feel that when we come to learn of our own resilience and inner strength, we become less reliant on fables and fanciful tales. We can appreciate them and even draw lessons from them. But we are not held helpless to the concept of them. How did my weary mortal mind postulate such a notion as this? In shortest terms, I survived.

I navigated a broken childhood fraught with mental insta-bility, disease, and the emotional manipulations of an unwitting mother, loss of loved ones and friends while serving as a soldier in the Canadian Armed Forces, and I navigated a world of death, dying, and disease as a paramedic in a decaying urban sprawl. I have seen death in all its various forms, and I have yearned for it by my own hand — yet I remain. I now live in a life replete with love, light, and laughter. All I had to do was find a little hope.

When I was seventeen, my mother received a phone call. It culminated in her bewailing and falling to the linoleum floor of the kitchen. She had received word that a dear family friend of ours had just died by way of suicide. His body was found in a park. He had hung himself. For obvious reasons, I will not use his real name. But what I will tell you is that this man, Leo, had been with our family through some of the most turbulent times of our existence.

I do not know how my mother first came to meet with Leo, but I know it was shortly after she had begun chemotherapy. She treated him like a son — one she loved very much. I was around nine, maybe ten when my mother was first diagnosed with cancer. She would sometimes come into my room late at night and tell me that she was tired, and did not want to allow treatments to continue. She told me that she wanted to die. She asked that I not worry because Leo would look after me.

My mother was a single parent, and Leo was a great guy, but the prospect of trading her life to go on and live with him was a prospect I cared very little for. My not wanting Leo as a surrogate caregiver was no reflection of him as a person; it was just the childish whims of a boy who wanted his mother to live forever.

As it came to be, my mother would undergo treatment, and she would beat cancer. Incredibly, she would have to wage this battle several more times over the span of her life, and my formative years. When my mother received the call about Leo, I had never seen her so disembodied by grief before. It was a peculiar sight to witness. At seventeen, I was not well equipped to manage such harrowing forms of grief, especially when navigating my own.

Leo dying by suicide was a shock to us all, and yet the concept of suicide was not. When I was approximately eleven, my mother had attempted to take her own life, resulting in her being airlifted to a hospital in the city. Afterward, my mother would often speak about the prospect of suicide as though it was a distant relative she yearned to see. It rested in front of her gaze on many long, lonely nights. It's a halting thing to observe as a son.

I once asked my mother how she would feel if she successfully ended her life, leaving me to wander the world as an orphan. She balked at me and demanded that I not be so "fucking selfish." That too is a halting contemplation for a son. When I was thirty-four, I would finally fall to my worst fears and become that orphan. My mother would die by suicide on a cold November morning just a month shy of her next birthday. She would leave behind a scathing three-page note, written by a tired hand. I could recite this terrible prose for you line by line via memory alone. I won't, of course. The note wasn't meant for you…

By the time my mother had passed, I had been working as a medic for many years. I have been to many suicides, I have read many notes, and my hands have touched the cold skin of so many lost souls. For a time, the prism through which I used to stare at the world was a shattered phantasmagoria of death and disease. To say it plainly, this was a depressing time of my life. The only respite came in the form of whiskey kisses and dimly lit barrooms. The warmth that alcohol gifted to my body was a welcomed reprieve from all the blood and tears that stained the creases of my dejected medic hands.

I lived with a soul full of ghosts. I could see them as baroquely as I view any living person. The difference being that their likeness not only stayed shackled to whatever street corner or apartment I had found them in or on, but they would hide in the shadows of my bedroom, or the steam that caressed my bathroom mirror. These were the early warning signs of PTSD. Signs I attempted to drink to oblivion. As it turns out, the demons of our soul can swim with lethal proficiency.

My days on ambulance came to an end when I was arrested for driving while intoxicated. My blood alcohol was well beyond the legal limit. I was arrested, charged, and convicted after pleading guilty without contestation. At the time, that felt like rock bottom for me. It wasn't. It was, however, a lesson in the true illusion of *rock bottom*. When you feel that you are at your deepest depths, I assure you, there is a layer beneath you that you should wish not to explore.

It was coming to that realization — that the descent of depression knows no bottomless bounds — from which an ironic hope was born. If life and its worst moments hold no measurement, then by universal law, the same must be true for happiness and prosperity. Depression is an anchor; hope, the catalyst of flight. From the Wright brothers to our souls, it's hope that lifts us.

In 2018, after many arduous hours spent sitting in a skilled therapist's office, I conceded to needing help, and I gave myself over to an addictions and rehabilitation program. Yielding control (even when we've lost it for ourselves and care not to admit it) is one of the most frightening prospects of the human condition. I feel that this is why it is so difficult to treat and thwart addiction among addicts. I have never met an addict who did not want help, but I have both been and met with plenty who are not ready for it. Handing over agency of ourselves to others is a frightful affair that can jostle even the utmost of stoic souls.

It was only when I was ready that I became willing. In that willingness came the embers of hope that have gone on to become a guiding light for me and my life. I have been to some disbelievingly hopeless places, introspectively and objectively. I have danced with death, smelled the foul whiskey on its breath, and I have risen from places I once deemed purgatory. I had to learn to accept loss, pain, grief, and self in order to move out from beneath the shadows of despair and into the warmth of life anew.

The greatest gift of a living life is that it is subject to change. Sometimes, we are blessed with flawless moments of jubilance. Other times, we are crippled beneath the heft of sorrow and anguish. But in coming to the understanding that nothing is forever, not even the darkest of skies or the densest of storm clouds, we can cultivate ways to move forward.

My journey started with an innocuous — but loathsome — blog post. A story I shared online about my struggles and my woes. I was surprised to wake with several messages in my inbox. They were from total strangers from varying parts of the world. They thanked me for writing and sharing parts of my story, and they went on to share aspects of their own. I started to believe that my story was not a unique one; it was merely uniquely mine. This led to an understanding that I am never as alone as I may feel.

In life, death is the only certainty. A cruel irony, I admit. If we are fortunate to live long enough and healthily enough, we are unquestionably going to have to endure pain and loss of some kind. Finding ways through is the key to unlocking tomorrow. Looking too far ahead, things become stressful, or seemingly insurmountable. Peering too far in the past, we miss what's in front of us.

Maintaining a present mind and empathetic heart are what I feel are the paradigms of growth and forward momentum. I wake up every morning, and before I let myself fall from bed to begin the many responsibilities of a day, I take inventory of what makes me grateful. For example: I came from a broken home, I have witnessed the death of family and friends, I once floundered in a tawny sea of scotch. And now, I wake to a house replete with joy and a woman I love, her two beautiful daughters, two dogs, and two zany cats.

The youngest little woman in our troop was diagnosed with type 1 diabetes when she was just five years old. Every day, she grants me examples of unwavering strength and positivity. Her everlasting smile and kind heart amid daily needles, glucose lows, and unknowns are pinnacle demonstrations that we are not products of what happens to us, but rather ambassadors of what life can be in spite of what we go through. I will always be grateful to that little girl and her immense courage.

This little life of mine, the one I now live, is only made possible by realizing that choice resides within me. I am not bound to any one moment in time; I am in charge of how I use and navigate said time. Time does not heal all wounds. I am still very much a wounded man — I am just no longer a hopeless one.

Time is a gift. Each day I am granted on this earth, in this life, I am overcome by a tremendous sense of appreciation and humility. When I learned that I was worthy of love, I found it. Accepting the loss of those I have loved paved the way to accepting that my love for them never fades. They do not need to be here in order for me to love them. I am allowed to miss them, and I do.

I miss my mum, my sister, the boys I served with, all of them. Some days I still cry. That's all right. Nothing is permanent. "*Grief spikes,*" my therapist calls them. Ride the wave. Eventually, seas settle down, and we reach the soft sand of the shorelines.

Knowing and accepting that I am allowed to have my moments of sadness along with the better times of smiles and laughs has been a transformative experience for me. In everything I do, there will forever be a slight melancholy inside of me. But sadness does not have to be the driving force of my existence, and my believing in that has become my greatest strength. I am a man who is blessed by a life I never thought possible. And so, I end this as if it were a letter:

My dearest Sheena, Olivia, Claire, Drew, Steven, and Amy, and so many more. Thank you for allowing a wretch like me to live in a wealth that makes me feel like the richest man alive. I did not wait for time to save me; I did, however, accept the right time to save myself!

First Place — Nonfiction

"Beyond Time's Reach", with its well-constructed sentences and beautiful use of language, but more importantly its exploration of loss and apathy and addiction, reminds us that true connection in writing is about uncertainty, risk, and emotional exposure. While the specific incidents described — a mother's suicide, drinking into oblivion, a DUI arrest — may not be universal, the emotions tied to them are. By detailing a broken childhood fraught with mental instability, disease, and manipulation, the author reminds us that vulnerability is not a sign of weakness, but rather an expression of courage and authenticity. This exquisite piece of

writing is not, however, merely a journey into the darkness. It is ultimately about hope. It reminds the reader that it is a privilege to have lived and loved and been in love. And that, as Leonard Cohen once penned, "There is a crack, a crack in everything. That's how the light gets in."

— Chris Brauer

A **House** of **Doors**

Pamela Medland

In my house there are many doors,
a version of me lives behind each one.
I've forgotten the way to half the doors
but some I stumble upon, some I search for.

I love the red doors best, their scarlet panels
blazing. My dead husband waits behind a blood gate,
wears ochre corduroys and a Cowichan sweater.
He laughs with me, dares *Do more.*

My grandfather lives behind carmine and yellow:
always warm, sometimes dashing. When I knock
on his door he answers smiling. Takes me
to the airport in his wide-winged car, winks
when my mother says she'll disown me for leaving.

I have trouble finding my grandmothers, they prefer
royal purple and teal. They appear and disappear, their doors
rare but haunting. I see them clearest when I am filled
with doubt.

My father's mother appears as a fan
dark-blue-painted silk on sandalwood.
My mother's mother is fleeting.
She shows an inch too much of leg,
speaks to me in French.
I watch them through a transom.

My favourite doors are azure.
I hover on their thresholds, float in and out.
Their locks are tricky and I'm often lost.
One day I'll die and stay on the inside looking out,
my children dappled by stained-glass hues of green and amber.

First Place — **Poetry**

The images in this piece captured my imagination as it made me contemplate my own doors.

— Sheri-D Wilson

Anything **Boys Can Do**

Angie Abdou

The gym is noisy and reeks of human sweat soaked deep into rubber mats. Loud voices bounce off the cement walls. Cassandra is shaken by waves of nostalgia. It's the sound and smell of her childhood. All she needs is her brother holding her down and burping in her face and she could be ten years old.

Six thick blue mats, big red circles in the centre, lay evenly throughout the gym, three then three. Two spandex-clad opponents grapple on each, scrapping to get a grip on the other's legs or arms. Thomas, her big brother, used to wrestle, and she's *too* well acquainted with the various holds, remembers clearly the feel of a chin piercing in the back of her thigh and an elbow jabbing her calf as he torqued her ankles, ignoring her pleas of "I give! I give!"

Now she and Thomas make their way to the wooden bleachers, checking the mats for Brock, Thomas's teenage son. Cassandra's business trip to Regina happened to coincide with Brock's Saskatchewan High School Championship.

"Plenty of room to sit. Not a popular sport," says Thomas, pointing to an open spot. "I didn't push Brock into it. He picked wrestling himself. What's wrong with golf? Make some money, save your joints." Thomas steers her into the middle of the second row where they'll have a clear view of the centre mat — Brock's on deck. "Or swimming? Hang out with girls in bathing suits instead of getting peed on in the shower by a bunch of brutes." Though Cassandra and Thomas sit close together, no one would mistake them for a couple. They look too much alike, blue eyes, sharp noses and chins, naturally messy hair. Thomas still has his black hair. Cassandra's curls have started to grey.

"There'd be money in wrestling if the Brockster went pro." Cassandra goes for her brother's Achilles heel, knows that professional wrestling — steroid-induced men in tights performing choreographed routines of violence — has little relation to the sport of Olympic wrestling, *real* wrestling. No relation at all as far as the Olympic wrestlers are concerned.

Thomas ignores her. "Check out the girl wrestlers, Cass. There's something new for you. Too bad girls didn't do it when we were kids — maybe you could've learned to defend yourself." He ruffles her hair as if she's still thirteen.

She knows he means "defend yourself against *me*" but she quickly moves her hand to cover a small dark bruise on her wrist, a thumbprint. It's nothing really, no big deal, but she knows she'd have a hard time convincing her brother. He's never liked her husband.

"Me wrestling? I can't imagine," she says quietly, looking toward the two young women, each struggling for a grip around her opponent's head. "I did like watching you guys, though. All those wins, all the trophies." Medals took the place of oxygen in their family home.

"Didn't you get sick of it? All the fuss?"

Again, she knows he means all the fuss *about me*. "Nah, everyone lives in someone's shadow. Yours wasn't such a bad one to be in." She pushes his shoulder. "Don't look so guilty. I was proud of you."

"Look at all the girl wrestlers. There are as many as boys!"

"Not necessarily a bad thing. Good for them. If guys can do it, why can't they do it?" Cassandra slides her coat under her butt. These benches are torture. She and her brother stare as two girls attack each other, each straining to force the other to the ground, losing their grip, slipping in each other's sweat.

"Geez." Thomas sounds disgusted. "Who wants to watch that? Gross."

Cassandra feels a rising heat and nausea that she associates with shame. "Why are they any more gross than boys wrestling? A handle is a handle. Male or female."

She knows the sport's rules and its language, knows that wrestlers get points from turning each other and anywhere they can get a grip to do so is a "handle." Under the arm, under the leg, in the crotch. Anywhere. A wrestler might use a hand, an arm, the neck, the head — any suitable lever. It's not unusual for one wrestler to put his head in the armpit or between the legs of another, using the strength of his neck to force an opponent to his back.

Cassandra's accustomed to all the body-on-body messiness of this sport, as is her brother. So what's the problem? "Sweaty wrestlers with their heads in each others' crotches never struck you as vulgar before." She readjusts her coat, the bench hard against her tailbone.

"It's never been eighteen-year-old women going at each other like wildcats. Look!" One female grappler wrenches another's upper body, slams her to the mat. The ref blows his whistle. Someone bleeds. Each combatant pulls a mandatory hanky from the front of her singlet and pats off her skin.

"Ugh." With that one grunt, Cassandra gives. She admits she's offended.

"And their hair," Thomas adds. Half in and half out of a ponytail, it's matted and tangled around the headgear they wear to keep their ears from getting battered and swollen. Cauliflower ears have apparently not caught on with the girls yet.

Cassandra looks away. Thomas's cauliflower ears are bad, even after all these years. She remembers when he was thirteen, good in his age group but still in awe of the national team guys. They all had mutilated ears — ear cartilage inflamed from the constant butting of heads, and then eventually hardened for good so that growths bulged from the top and ear canals swelled almost shut. Cauliflower ears. Thomas's heroes. When his own ears started to swell, he'd pinch and rub them, working on his own cauli.

In high school, though, he hated people staring. When anyone asked what happened to his ears, he'd snap, "They melted in a fire."

The girls' match heats up. Cassandra still won't look, but she can't help hearing the cheers.

"Take her down, Janice. She's all yours!"

"Shoot for the crotch, Mary! Shoot!"

Thomas elbows her in the side, smirking and tilting his head toward the offending mat.

"Well, it's certainly not how Mom and Dad taught me how to behave," she concedes. "But new generation, new rules, new roles."

A herd of boys Brock's age file into the row behind them. She hears them mention Brock. They smell of sweat and vinegar and have pig-farm breath. Cassandra knows cutting weight brings on the breath: a week of dehydration followed by a full day of wrestling. The vinegar helps fight ringworm, the plague of the mats.

"Hey, Brock's up now." Thomas is jumpy and chews on the knuckle of his right thumb. "Against that strong kid from a farm just outside of Swift Current." Cassandra follows his gaze. Brock's about to begin his match, but as he moves to centre ring, the ref shakes his head and pushes a palm into Brock's chest. The table judges signal the girls to move onto this mat instead.

"Damn!" Thomas is really keyed up. "The girls' tournament must be behind. We'll be here forever."

The teens behind them fidget. "Aw, shit. It's just chicks wrestling. Let's go outside and come back to see the *real* finals."

"Yeah, unless they're wrestling in mud or jelly, I don't need to see it."

Cassandra tries not to listen. She watches Brock instead, then his rival. Both boys have fought hard to make it to this semi-final. The other wrestler looks brutal. His ear is patched with bloody tape, he has a soaked tampon shoved up his nose. He bounces up and down, then from one foot to the other, leaning his head toward his coach, who pantomimes an underhook while whispering instructions in his battered ear. The kid fingers his nostril, checking whether the blood has seeped through his tampon.

Thomas pokes Cassandra, pointing at the current match. A young medic bandages up one girl's head as blood runs toward her eye. Thomas whispers but his tone isn't soft. "*This* should *not* be allowed."

"Wrestling is ugly. No matter who's doing it."
He's silent.
"You're the one who said golf's better. Or swimming."

Thomas shushes her. Brock has taken off his sweatpants. He jumps knees to chest three times and then hits the palm of his hand to his face, hard three times, as if to wake himself with violence. Then he heads to the centre ring. He and his opponent face each other, their lean bodies taut, their faces grim. Each pulls a hanky out of the front of his singlet, shows it to the ref, tucks it back in place. The ref then looks to Brock, who holds out both arms. The ref runs a hand over each, checking for sweat or oil, anything slippery. He quickly runs his hand over Brock's fingernails too, then turns to the other boy. The ref nods. The whistle blows.

"This match is the tournament," says Thomas. "The other pool is weak. The final will be a cakewalk."

Brock is big for his age, it's the 180-pound weight class, but the other boy is bigger. A farm kid with blazing red hair. Still, Brock's probably quicker. And, if he's anything like his father, meaner — not afraid to dig a thumb into his opponent's face, or his chin into the spine, not afraid to go a bit against the joint when the ref has an awkward view. "He bit my fucking ball sack" — a decades-old accusation, never confirmed but one Cassandra will always remember.

Brock gets the farm kid's leg. He holds it up while the boy struggles for balance. Then Brock uses his right foot to sweep the boy's other leg out from under him. They fall to the mat with a loud thud. The redhead manages to twist, though, and they both land stomach down. Still, Brock lands on top. One point Brock.

Thomas squirms in his seat, as if he's the one going for each hip toss, each single leg, each foot sweep.

Brock wraps both arms around his opponent's waist. The gut wrench. He'll squeeze his arms and then torque. If the redhead's back turns to the mat, Brock will get two points. Wrestlers break ribs trying not to get flipped. A groan. Brock or the farm kid? Cassandra can't tell. Another groan and they turn, the boy's feet flung in the air as Brock arches him through. Three-nothing Brock.

"Okay, good." Thomas relaxes a little but still chews his thumb. "This guy is good, though. Strong and explosive. Brock can't let up."

He never pushes Brock? He'd rather Brock didn't wrestle? She bites the inside of her cheeks.

Cassandra notices a female wrestler, pulling sweatpants over her spandex suit, her face purple with bruises, a bleeding wound above her eye. The beaten girl is intent on Brock's match, cheering loudly. His girlfriend? Cassandra nudges Thomas. He flinches at the girl's swollen face.

"Once we would've assumed a man had done that to her," Cassandra says as if to herself. "Women's lib. Now we can do it to each other."

"Women's lib," Thomas snorts.

Cassandra ignores him, turns her attention back to Brock's match. Both wrestlers stand, the farm boy almost a full head taller. "Go Brock," she yells. "Just two more minutes! Hang in there!"

"You got him, Brockster!" Thomas seconds.

Neither boy can get a good hold of the other, so they still stand, grappling for position. Brock is too fast, won't let the other guy get his legs. The other guy is too strong, hard to do anything with even when Brock does get a tight hold on his limbs. They bump chests and Brock gets trapped in a bear hug.

"Shit!" Cassandra and Thomas jump to their feet.

The redhead arches his back, lifting Brock off his feet. Chest to chest. At the breaking point, the farm kid twists and they both fall, Brock on his back. Three points all.

Thomas shuts his eyes and falls back to his seat. "No."

Brock edges out of bounds and the ref blows his whistle for the wrestlers to stand. Tied match. Cassandra's ears ring, the crowd's screaming so loud.

And she's as loud as anyone. "C'mon Brock! Go!!"

The match winds down to the last minute, both boys getting scrappier. Foreheads pressed together, they dip and bend, trying to get a hold of each other's arms or legs.

"Eeeeeeeeee!" A shriek cuts through the thunderous cheers.

Which one of them yelled?

Brock. He holds his hand over his left eye, waves the referee to blow the whistle and drops to his knees. The crowd murmurs, spectators chattering on, while Brock shields his eye. The ref tries to pry Brock's hand away to get a look.

"Brock's got him," a boy in the row behind Cassandra says. "He'll shake this off."

"And he's got the staying power. He finishes hard. The last half —"

Brock wails, cutting off the chattering. Not a scream, not a cry, but a continuous, piercing wail. Everyone strains to see what's happened. All hush as Brock's opponent bends, leans over him slowly, tentatively. Then he rears up, one hand on his stomach, the other to his forehead. He's just a kid, Cassandra remembers. A big, scared kid.

Brock's opponent yells at his coach. Cassandra struggles to make out his words. "… eye… in his… his… his eye is in his hand!" The boy starts to pace, frantically back and forth. Even from this distance, Cassandra can tell he's crying.

Everything moves too slow, not making sense. Brock's eye? In his hand?

A young woman rushes to the middle of the mat, carrying a medical bag. She bends over Brock and then rears up just as fast as the kid did. She presses a hand to her moth, but recovers quickly, squats beside Brock.

Cassandra squeezes Thomas's knee. Hands in his hair, he rocks. Back and forth. Back and forth. She takes a deep breath and heads down, leaving Thomas with his head in his hands. She crosses the floor with such authority that no one questions her.

Brock's eyeball isn't really out. The lid has been pushed all the way underneath, so the eye, the full ball of it, looks to be bulging out of his face. "It's me, Brock, Auntie Cass. Let me see. You're going to be okay." She remembers this from Red Cross swimming lessons: say *You're going to be okay, everything will be fine.* No matter what.

"Auntie Cass, what's wrong? My eye. It hurts!" He whimpers, sounding so much younger than he looked in the middle of the mat with his tough, set face. "I thought I just poked it. Just a normal poke. But then I tried to blink, and I couldn't. I thought it was stuck. But then I thought if my eye is stuck open, why can't I see." He's talking fast. "Then I went like this." He gestures, holding his cupped hand toward his eyeball. Cassandra pinches her lips against the hard wave of nausea. "To see if my eye was there. I could feel it. Feel the whole thing."

"You're going to be okay, Brocky. Everything will be fine." She presses her nephew's face, tries to feel if the back of the eyeball still sits in its socket. The medic looks teary-eyed and more than happy to let Cassandra take over. The face-battered girl has rushed over to them, hovers, biting her lip and shifting foot to foot.

"I think we pull this skin out," Cassandra says. "It's just stuck underneath." She looks over her shoulder where the coach shrugs and nods. The medic too. Both hang back.

"Okay, hold on, Brocky. It'll just take a second." Cassandra presses her index finger firmly on the skin around Brock's eye, and yanks. It gives, then slides back into place. Brock blinks. Rubs his eye. Blinks again.

"There. Everything back where it's supposed to be. Piece of cake." Adrenaline races through Cassandra but she keeps her voice from shaking.

Brock shudders, shakes it off, and makes a move to stand.

"Nice sport." Cassandra glares at the coach. She wants to be mad at someone.

"Boys will be boys. You gonna keep going, Brockster?"
For God's sake.

The ref wags two fingers in front of Brock and then gives the nod.

Cassandra can just hear the kids. "He popped his eye out and kept wrestling. He's *that* tough." Fine line between tough and stupid.

She marches back to Thomas. As she gets to their spot in the bleachers, she hears the whistle. She won't watch the last minute. Thomas gets up and brushes past her. She can't read his face. She drops to the seat, eyes following her brother. What's he up to?

With the same performance of authority when Cassandra stormed the floor, Thomas strides to the coach in Brock's corner, leans over, mouth moving next to the coach's ear. The coach shoves him aside and yells to Brock. "Right leg's open. Single leg!"

Thomas rushes the referees' table. The men dressed in white look up, startled. Nod. The middle one stands, blows a whistle. The boys freeze. They whirl to their coaches and to the ref. What's happening? Only thirty seconds on the clock. The match tied.

The table ref takes the centre of the mat now. He raises the redhead's hand.

Brock stomps his foot so hard that Cassandra feels it in the stands. "What? No way!" She's lip-reading. Brock appeals to his coach, but the coach has spotted Thomas at the referees' table and slumps in his seat, defeated.

"No way! Get serious!" Brock turns from his coach to the ref and back again. "I got him! We're not done! I can win!"

The coach shrugs, points at Thomas. "Talk to him, son."

Brock goes right for his father, straight-arms him in the chest.

Thomas raises both hands in surrender. He throws an arm around Brock's shoulder, but Brock pushes it off.

The next semi-final has already started, diverting the crowd's attention. Brock shoves his dad again, a hand weakly meeting Thomas's chest. A child's gesture.

Cassandra turns away, blinking, stroking the bruise on her wrist. When she looks back, Brock has slumped, has given into his dad's hug. And finally the tears come.

A Letter to **My Love**

Annie Dearing

Hello, my darlin',

It's been a while since last we spoke. I miss our daily chats: while we were cooking or eating dinner or coming and going about the day.

The leaves are blowing now, my dear. I still see you out there working, cursing them all, and loving every minute. We once built a house with no trees, no leaves, no work. But then we found this beauty that gave us the green and the gold and the time to enjoy it, we thought.

The snow was on the mountain today; six weeks to go, you'd say, until it comes to us. I'll watch it for you to see if you are right this time, probably so. I'll bring in the wood to make the fires for comfort on winter nights; my job now is to build them so I am learning as I go. I didn't really watch before, so I now stumble along and keep a watchful eye.

I walk outdoors when I can, feeling the wind and the sun, and keeping apace of younger folk. I want to stay healthy to be here with our children, to give them comfort and share their sorrow. They don't know they are the ones who keep me strong and fierce.

Each day I find something to do, something to learn, since I have to buck up and accept the now. Others offer to help me, but I can't explain all the bits you knew by intuition and silent agreement. How can I explain what I really don't understand? So put your hand on my hand and show me what to do one last time.

We didn't start life easy, each of us rejected by a parent who could not love, always second best or less, by far. We grew up to adulthood together and held each other up.

The years without children could have broken us; the drugs, the tests, the surgeries that never worked. Then the dashed hopes of early positives, followed by disappointment. In those days, there was no support, no chat, nothing but depression for two. You never faltered, never stopped believing, and you were right.

We wanted our own family, to do things right; to be a haven for our children. We brought each babe into the circle of our love and friendship to be a part of the whole that would be our all, our brood.

Yesterday, there was a noise at the back door. For just a moment, I thought you were coming home. When I went to look, something had fallen, but just for a moment, I thought it was you.

I had a dream that we were walking together in a crowd, and I got ahead of you when you stopped to talk. I called to you and you kept getting farther and farther behind until I couldn't see you any more. It was much like this transition we are going through now.

They think that I can let you go without a whimper. But I have whimpered, I have wailed, I have whined, and you are still gone, and I am still here. You were my *anam cara*, my soul friend, and often my sole friend, who really got me and understood where I came from and where I was going.

You asked me to read to you that day, something you had never done before. I thought I couldn't do it, but I did and it calmed you. It didn't matter that it was *Game of Thrones* with ogres and castles. It was another conversation without the details and thoughts, just the sound of voices.

I can't deny that you are gone since I was with you. I sat with you, stroked your brow, hand on your heart as the breaths came farther and farther apart, each one seeming to be the last until finally it was.

The house is empty, and the cupboard is full but I am moving on, one foot in front of the other. The transition from we to me is painful but needed. I will make it for me but also for you to keep your memory strong and dear, always in our hearts.

Editor's Selection

The **Canary's** Cry

Jack Dowd

"What inspection?" Tina asked, slamming the last safety bar into place.

Clang.

"Since that kid knocked himself out last week, the whole park's being inspected," Lexi said.

Tina grunted and pulled a lever on the control panel. The waiting cart jerked forwards, the passengers screaming as they disappeared into the first curve.

A second cart entered the platform from the opposite direction, its nine riders drenched. Lexi walked alongside, unlocking each safety bar and releasing the passengers.

Clang. Clang. Clang.

"And everyone's getting inspected?" Tina asked.

"Yeah, everyone in the park." Lexi pushed the empty cart along the rails to Tina, who ushered the next riders onto the loading platform.

"Do we know when?" She watched as a little boy, boarding the cart with his mother, eyed the animatronic canary perched above the ride's entrance as it squawked. Once the passengers had taken their seats, Tina locked each safety bar on the cart.

Clang. Clang. Clang.

"We don't know. Mr. Cainwright just said it was happening soon."

Tina nodded and deployed the cart onto the circuit. The little boy squealed and clutched his mother as the cart rolled out of view.

Tina had always thought that the Canary's Cry was rather extreme for a children's ride. Mr. Cainwright had once described it as having a loose Wild West theme, with the carts painted to resemble runaway mine trucks and the crew forced to wear cowboy hats. Tina had long since abandoned hers, and had never seen Mr. Cainwright wearing his. The track had been laid in a figure eight, running directly over the entrance queue after the carts passed the first bend. If the giant canary eyeing passing riders wasn't intimidating enough, the track continued into a flooded mineshaft, drenching the riders before running at a forty-five-degree angle, dubbed the twisting track, before returning to the loading platform.

The canary's shrieks seemed louder today, as did the carts that rumbled overhead. Tina tried to ignore the pounding in her head. She hadn't believed Mr. Cainwright when he said they were expecting a surge of visitors, but after the injured child's mother had been interviewed by the local news team, the number of thrill seekers had doubled.

Mr. Cainwright was correct when he said any publicity was good publicity.

"Isn't that your boyfriend?" Lexi asked.

Tina looked up from the controls. Danny, his Afro making him appear taller than most of the crowd, was waving his arms from the middle of the queue. His shouts were lost to her, masked by the relentless thundering of the carts snaking above, but not to those around him.

"Ex-boyfriend. We broke up the other day, actually. We're still mates, though," Tina added, glancing at the controls. The nearest cart was approaching the flooded mineshaft, sixty seconds away from the loading platform.

"I'll be right back."

"What? No. Wait —"

Tina didn't let her finish. Ignoring Lexi's objections, she sprinted into the throng of waiting riders and began to weave her way under the wooden crowd barriers towards Danny. She dismissed the grumbling of the crowd with a smile and darted around the support beams to position herself opposite her ex-boyfriend.

Danny had not shaved that morning, and combined with the dark patches of skin under his eyes, Tina could believe he hadn't slept either. Chances were he'd been up all night playing Xbox with his mates.

"Let me skip the queue." Danny's breath smelt like liquorice, no doubt from the sweets he'd been scoffing at the gift shop. Tina wondered if she had left her staff discount card at his flat.

"I can't."

"Yeah, you can. Take me to the front."

"I can't. You know I can't."

Tina heard Lexi unlocking the passengers' safety bars and ushering them to the exit. *Clang. Clang. Clang.*

"C'mon," Danny pleaded.

Tina looked back at the platform. The last of the riders were disappearing down the exit ramp. Lexi was now shunting the empty cart forwards.

"For God's sake, fine! C'mon, then." She grabbed his arm and, ignoring the outcries, dragged him around the support beam and back through the mass of people.

"Sit," she demanded when they reached the platform and Danny happily clambered into the front row of the nearest cart.

She allowed the next riders to position themselves around Danny before adjusting their safety bars.

"How many times can I ride?" Danny asked.

Clang. Clang. Clang.

"Just once," Tina said, returning to the controls.

She pulled the lever and watched Danny and the other riders scream as the cart entered the first curve.

"Sorry, but it's easier if I just let him do it, y'know? He'll stop nagging me then. Otherwise he'll go on and on about it."

Tina turned to find Mr. Cainwright, his bald head gleaming in the sun, glaring at her from the end of the platform.

•

"What'd he say then?"

Tina didn't answer Lexi immediately. Instead, she continued to frown at her blank phone screen. No missed calls or notifications from Danny.

"He said if the inspector saw me, I'd be fired on the spot." She shrugged. "You got a drink?"

The sounds of the ride were muffled from the staff room in the portacabin, but they were still loud enough to worsen Tina's headache. She searched the cramped space for a discarded drink but found none.

"No. I had mine at lunch. I tried that new bubble tea thing they were doing at the kiosk.

"C'mon," Lexi said, "we're due back on now."

Tina grunted, pocketed her phone, and followed Lexi through the door and along a metal walkway back towards the loading platform. When they returned, Tina was dismayed to discover that the crowd had seemingly doubled over their lunch break. The queue had surpassed the robotic canary and zigzagged away between the support beams and towards the park entrance. Their lunch relief, two teenage boys Tina didn't remember the names of nor cared to learn, silently left, delighted to escape the monotonous work.

When the park's closing bell sounded several hours later, Tina was delighted to see Mr. Cainwright raising a closed sign at the end of the queue. The waiting riders had shrunk to thirty people, but as her boss turned to leave, she spotted a familiar figure dipping under the sign.

"Tina…" Lexi said.

"I know. I can see him. It's Danny."

"No, I need the loo."

"What?"

"I really need to go. Like, seriously. Now."

"But we'll be finished in a minute."

Lexi seemed to be swaying on the spot, almost dancing. Her eyes kept darting to the exit. "I'll be quick then, yeah? It's that bubble tea thing."

Before Tina could respond, Lexi sprinted down the exit ramp and disappeared.

Tina swore and slammed the safety bars of the waiting cart.

Clang. Clang. Clang.

If he costs me my job, I swear I'll kill him, she thought. She deployed the cart and another took its place.

Clang. Clang. Clang.

She examined the fresh passengers as they took their seats. None of them looked like an inspector. Now that he was closer to the platform, Tina could see that Danny held something red in his hands.

Clang. Clang. Clang.

She watched the cart rattle out of the platform before a new one rolled into view.

What's he holding?

Clang. Clang. Clang.

"Hey," Danny said as the other riders clambered into the cart. In his hand was a single scarlet rose. "You all right?"

Tina failed to find the words to answer him.

"Look, I'm sorry about earlier on, yeah? I heard afterwards there was an inspector around. I didn't know. Here." Tina accepted the offered rose and placed it on the controls, unsure what else to do with it. She locked the bars on the waiting cart, unable to look at her former boyfriend.

Clang. Clang. Clang.

"You all right?" Danny asked again.

"No one's given me flowers before," Tina said. She sent the final cart of thrill seekers onto the circuit.

"Is there time for one last ride for me then?"

"You want to go on it… again?"

The spell was broken.

"Yeah, there was a stupid girl sitting behind me who wouldn't stop screaming the whole time. I think I'm actually half deaf now."

A cart of drenched riders came into view. "Yeah. Yeah, fine." She unlocked the passengers and rolled the cart forward.

Clang. Clang. Clang.

"Get in."

"Cheers, babe."

She dodged his attempt at a kiss, back-stepped to the controls, and pulled the release lever. The cart jerked forwards into the first bend.

Danny screamed something as he swept into the first bend but the wind stole his words. Tina studied the rose, turning it over in her hands. It was plastic, bore a label from the park's gift shop, and had the price tag of four pounds ninety-nine.

"Christina!"

Mr. Cainwright was approaching, weaving his way through the crowd barriers. A middle-aged man in a suit followed him.

Tina searched the platform in the hope that Lexi had returned. She hadn't.

"This is our park inspector, Mr. Tillman. He'd like to share his report with you," Mr. Cainwright said.

Tina summoned a smile and peered at the controls as the two men reached the platform. Danny's cart was nearing the first drop.

"Christina, a pleasure to meet you," Mr. Tillman said. "I visited earlier this morning, at around noon. You were here with your friend…"

"Lexi," Mr. Cainwright interrupted, looking down the platform. Tina noticed his eyes linger over the plastic rose.

Danny screamed as his cart rattled overhead and disappeared towards the flooded mineshaft.

"Yes, Lexi," Mr. Tillman continued. "Anyway, I have the report here."

Tina spared the controls a final glance. Danny was in the splash zone while the remaining carts rattled back into the platform.

"I'm delighted to say that we have exciting news," the inspector smiled. "We just wanted to know if you would consider a promotion to a ride manager. Until we can find a permanent solution."

"Oh."

She heard Danny's cart racing across the twisting track.

"Christina, is there anyone on that?" Mr. Cainwright asked. "Where's Lexi?"

Tina didn't answer. She turned away from her boss, her back to the tracks, as Danny's cart trundled back to the platform.

"Is there a problem?" Mr. Tillman asked.

"No. I didn't realize Christina had sent out an empty cart. We normally send one out at the start and end of each day to check the condition of the track. Good job, Christina."

Tina spun around. Danny's cart was empty. The safety bars were up.

Honourable Mention — Fiction

In "The Canary's Cry," we get a great crescendo of tension, but what I love about this piece is the knife-twist at the end. The tension building from the beginning turns out to be nothing compared to what's in store for the protagonist.

— David Brown

It Depends on **How You Look** at It

Charlotte Blair

Remembering always to breathe
isn't as easy as Thich says,
decoding the shadows of madness,
your tigers that live in the corners,
that aren't visible to everyone.
You don't dare to recognize
the facts as you breathe them.
Let them wrestle your wild
bones over meat,
let those images be, like stones
sidle through your fingers,
the bitter grit of life.
These moments firefly flash, watch
when you can't wait anymore,
when you sing,
So hard to be crazy
when you sing,
when you won't wait anymore.
These moments firefly flash — watch
the sweet grit of life
sidle through your fingers.

Let those images go like stones,
meat over bones.
Let your wild wrestle
those facts as you breathe them.
You dare to recognize
they aren't visible to everyone,
her tigers that live in the corners.
Decoding the shadows of madness
is as easy as Thich says —
remembering always to breathe.

Honourable Mention — Poetry

I liked the tempo of this piece, and how it brought me to the very place it was describing.

— Sheri-D Wilson

The **Stanley Cup** Caper

Robert J. Sawyer

"She shoots! She scores! For the first time in sixty-seven years, the Toronto Maple Leafs have won the Stanley Cup! Captain Karen Lopez and her team have skated to victory as the 2031 NHL champions. The hometown crowd here is going wild, and — wait! Wait! Ladies and gentlemen, this is incredible ... we've just received word that the Stanley Cup trophy is missing!"

Detectives Joginder Singh and Trista Chong let their car drive them east along the Gardiner Expressway. At Bathurst, the vehicle headed down into the tunnel. Jo shuddered; he hated the underground portion of the Gardiner. Sadly, his fear of tunnels also kept him from using the subway, even though it now ran all the way from Pearson Airport to the Pickering Solar Power Plant.

Still, the one tolerable thing about going underground here was that he didn't have to lay eyes on the spire of the Quebec Consulate; Trista, fifteen years his junior, didn't really remember a united Canada, but Jo certainly did.

At Yonge, their car resurfaced. South of them was the *Toronto Sun-Star* building. But they were going north: their car let them out across the street from the Hockey Hall of Fame. Of course, there was no place to park; the car would just keep driving around the block until they signalled it to pick them up.

Jo and Trista had spent most of yesterday fruitlessly examining the crime scene at the WestJet Centre. Today, they were going to start by having a look at the duplicate Stanley Cup — the mock-up that was on public display at the Hall of Fame — just to get a feel for the dimensions of the stolen object.

Once inside, Jo stood in front of the glass case containing the duplicate, while Trista walked around the case, taking pictures of the duplicate's engraved surface with her pocketbrain. When she was finished, something apparently caught her eye. "Look!" she crowed, pointing to the adjacent glass case. "There it is — taken apart, but there it is!"

Jo glanced at the other case and laughed. "Those are just retired bands."

Trista made a perplexed frown. "Like the Barenaked Ladies?"

"No. Bands from the original trophy. It always consists of the cup on top and five circular bands forming the cylindrical body." He pointed back at the mock-up. "See? Each of the five bands has room for listing the members of thirteen winning teams. When they fill the last spot on the bottom band, they retire the top one, slide the other four up, and add a new band. Those bands in that other case are the ones that have already been removed."

Trista took some pictures of the retired bands, then looked back at the mock-up, peering at its base. "But the last band on the trophy is already full," she said.

Jo nodded. "That's right. They're going to have to retire the top band this year and start a new one." He paused. "Seen enough?"

Trista nodded. They exited, crossed the street, and waited for their car to come get them. With the Gardiner buried, it was easy to see the Central Nanotechnology Tower on the lakeshore, but there was no point going up to the observation deck anymore. Jo shook his head; he was old enough to remember when the city's nickname had been Hogtown, not Smogtown.

The car took them north on Yonge Street, the toll being debited automatically. It had been ten years since GTA amalgamation, combining Toronto with everything from Mississauga to Oshawa. Still, the stolen trophy had to be somewhere inside the supercity's borders; like every other North American metropolis, T.O. was surrounded by security checkpoints, and something as big as the Stanley Cup couldn't have been smuggled out.

On their left now was the Eaton Centre. Jo's sister had a condominium there, in what had once been a Grand & Toy store; with most people shopping online these days, there was little need for big malls. As they continued up Yonge, the towers of Ryerson — "the Harvard of the North," as CNNMSNBC had recently dubbed it — were visible off to the right. Jo watched the landscape going by — a succession of Tim Hortons donut shops, pot bars, and licensed bordellos. Trista, meanwhile, had her pocketbrain out and was staring at its screen, studying the pictures she'd taken earlier.

Their car turned right onto Carleton, heading towards Maple Leaf Gardens — a historic site, which perhaps might hold a clue — when suddenly Trista looked up from her screen. "No! Car, turn around — head to University Avenue and then go south."

Jo looked at his partner. "What's up?"

"I think I know where the Stanley Cup is."

"Where?"

Trista brought up a map of downtown Toronto on her pock-etbrain and showed it to him. "Right there," she said, tapping a spot on the screen.

"Oh, come on!" said Jo. "Why would they want it?"

"Did you see what was on that band they're going to retire this year?"

"Thirteen old winning teams," said Jo.

"Yes — but which teams?"

"I have no idea."

She brought up one of the images she'd taken of the dupli-cate trophy. "The winners from 1953 to 1965."

"So?"

"So I've read what's on all the bands now, including the retired ones. The band they're about to remove lists the only five-wins-in-a-row Stanley Cup champions."

"Really?"

"Yes. See? From 1956 through 1960, Montreal won the Stan-ley Cup every single year, and —"

Jo got it in a flash. "And there's no way a sovereign Quebec would let the band commemorating that be archived at the Hockey Hall of Fame, which is on Canadian soil. But the Que-bec Consulate — "

"Exactly!" said Trista. "The Quebec Consulate is technically Québecois soil."

Jo frowned. "But we don't have any jurisdiction on the con-sulate grounds."

"I know," said Trista. "It'll take some political wrangling between Ottawa and Quebec."

"*Plus ça change, plus c'est la même chose,*" said Jo.

"What's that mean?" asked Trista. She was young enough that she hadn't had to study French in school.

Jo looked out the car's window as they turned onto University, passing the statue of Mel Lastman. "The more things change," he said, "the more they stay the same."

Rainy Day **Treasures**

Jill Martin

The rain, the first in a month, had started falling hours before I awoke. Now, lingering over a second cup of coffee, I watched the water cascade over the rim of the birdbath and splash on the flowerbed below. We needed the rain, I conceded.

Breaking the cycle of daily busyness, rainy days scurry us into a temporary hibernation where, cocooned safe and dry from the streaming wet, we cave dwellers yearn to burrow into the tunnels of the past. The older I get, the louder that past knocks on the windows of my present. An invitation to leave a legacy, if you will, with those who will come after.

Over many decades, my various collections had fallen victim to rainy day burrowing. Dormant in basements or crawl spaces, one by one, the pillars of my past found themselves ignominiously chucked to the curb. My most sacred memorabilia, things I would take if given an evacuation order, had been reduced to a mere two boxes. *Jill's Treasures.* One houses my diaries, beginning in 1961. The second, sacred trivia like my Central Collegiate school directories, September Frosh schedule, my special coins and stamps, a string tie Crown Royal bag and a blue Ponytail treasure box.

Equipped with a sliding lock apparatus, the Ponytail box was a Christmas gift from my parents. A teenager, who I liked to imagine was me, dances across the pale sky-blue lid, a Top 40 tune blaring on the record player beside her.

My first collection was a pile of comic books, higher than I was tall, stacked behind the couch. After Christmas and a 64 pack of Crayola crayons, my art filled my first canvas — the wall behind the couch. Such etchings did not sit well with my mother, even though I secretly knew I had inherited the troublesome *Gotta Keep It* gene from her.

By the time I entered kindergarten, Mom had filled one banana box with my 'art': strange beasts, pink clouds floating in a purple sky, and circles. Circle after circle. Red, blue, and yellow. Like most toddlers, I hung the sun from the upper right corner, rays strafing the horizon below. I have but a few of those hundreds of paintings, but the ones I have kept never fail to transport me to my growing-up years on the prairies. To a simpler time.

When I started elementary school, Mom nabbed a second banana box from the grocery store in which to hoard my masterpieces. By grade three, art had deferred to stamps, postcards of kittens, playing cards, anything colourful and tradable on the school playground. Over the years and especially on rainy days, I would sift through the boxes of those eclectic treasures.

Today, though, I had special plans with my grandson, Nik.

"Time to get at it," I said, eyeing the droplets hurrying down the windowpane. "Tide and time, you know."

I lugged my second evacuation box from the garage and set it beside the chair by the living room window, where I sat mesmerized by the rain pummelling the red salvia blooms in the front flowerbed. The bees had buggered off, hoping for better nectar-gathering weather tomorrow.

The wide armchair was old and well worn, the grey plaid less vibrant and the soft velour less plush. If it might speak, the chair would have many stories to tell. My children had nestled beside me as they grew up, wide-eyed at the stories I read to them, sniffling after scraping their knees on the driveway, or frightened at the thunder that shook the windowpanes.

My grandson loved the old chair — the storytelling chair, he called it.

I looked up at the sound of a car. The silver SUV turned sharply into the driveway, tires cutting through a wall of water. My grandson, Nik, slammed the passenger door of the car and hopscotched toward the house through the pounding rain. Like me, Nik loved rainy days.

"Hi, sweetheart. Don't take off your shoes. Gotta get the recycling to the curb. They come in an hour."

Without a second thought, Nik walked to the bag and heaved it over his shoulder. I pushed the garage door opener.

"Hurry, dear. It's really coming down."

"Whoa, Nanny. What's all the clinking?" Nik asked as he lugged the bag across the garage floor.

"Just the glass bottles. We had quite a few this week."

"Too bad they have to break perfectly good bottles."

"Well, I suppose they melt them down and make new ones."

"Yeah, I guess. Why not just reuse them?"

Nik has been a questioning child. Questions stacked upon questions. I loved his inquisitive nature. Now, with his entrance into junior high, his interests had expanded.

"Guess I'll need to change," Nik giggled. He yanked the shirt out of his jeans and squeezed it with both hands. A steady stream of water puddled on the garage floor.

"No worries, sweetie. I've a drawer full of clothes for such emergencies."

"I love pro-D days, Nanny, 'cause I get to spend them with you. I brought my Pokémon collection. I've got some new ones and two rare premiums."

From an early age, Nik had exhibited the telltale signs of the family's rare but infamous collector gene. "Come on Nanny, come see," he would say, grabbing my fingers and leading me to his room. From seashells discovered on sunny beaches, to lava from Hawaii's Kona volcano, enough stuffies on his bed to fill a zoo, to binders full of trading cards, he knelt beside me, sharing his treasures.

Today, we would be partners in collector crime. A whole day digging into what Nik called *the old stuff*.

"Fancy a glass of chocolate milk?"

Glass in one hand and cookie in the other, Nik settled in the oversized chair.

"What's in the box, Nanny?"

"You'll see."

While Nik sipped his chocolate milk, I lifted the Crown Royal bag out of the box and placed it on the table. Nik eyed the velvet bag but didn't touch it. With treasure, anticipation was part of the thrill.

I squirmed my thumbs into the cinched knot, then pulled the gold cords aside and upended the bag.

"What are these, Nanny?" Nik asked, dipping his hands into the pile of strange paper circles.

"Milk bottle caps. Pogs. We collected and traded them. *Palm for a Silverwood. Purity for a Palm.*" The memory whisked me back to the playground, the wind ruffling my skirt and swirling withered leaves around my legs.

"So, when you were a kid, milk came in bottles?"

"Yes. Milk came in quart — that's a bit more than a litre — glass bottles. The top of the bottle was covered with shiny crimped foil. I remember thinking they looked like up-side-down parachutes."

Nik turned a couple of pogs between his fingers.

"The real gems, though, the tradable items, were those milk caps. They sat on a glass lip ringing the top of the bottle. There was a tab, sort of like a pull tab on a pop can, in the centre of the cap. The name of the dairy and its logo were printed above the tab. When the bottle was empty, I'd snag the cap and add it to my collection."

"So your mom let you keep them?"

"Of course. Everyone collected them, and everyone kept them in a Crown Royal bag. Palm Dairy milk caps were the most common, but I had some rare ones from Silverwood, Purity, and Co-op Dairies."

Nik paused, deep in thought, a couple of pogs in his hand, watching the rain sheet the window.

"Did you have chocolate milk when you were growing up? I love chocolate milk." He took a lip-moustaching sip to prove his claim.

"Yes, we did, but only as a special treat. Here's a thought. Where do you think we bought our milk when I was a girl?"

Incredulous, perhaps, at such a ridiculous question, Nik's face erupted in a grin. "From the grocery store, of course, Nanny. Where else?"

"Nope. Milk was delivered right to our house through a cupboard built into the wall by the back door. Pretty handy, especially during cold Saskatchewan winters. One door faced the street. Another opened into the kitchen. Our favourite was Topsy chocolate."

"That's a funny name, Nanny."

"Funny or not, it was delicious. Every morning, Evan Shaw, our delivery man, picked up the empty glass bottle Mom had placed in the cupboard the night before. He left a quart of milk, maybe a small jar of Creamo, and sometimes the prized chocolate milk. Mom put the money in an empty Keen's dry mustard tin."

"I don't think that would be safe, Nanny. Anybody could steal it."

"That's where you're wrong, lovey. In all the years we lived on Normandy Avenue, our milk money was never filched."

How different my childhood street was from his twenty-first century paranoid avenue of alarms and security cameras. Unlocked doors, kids running everywhere, and door-to-door milk delivery, a product of its time, a time etched in order and predictability. Fitted only with a latch, any thief could have helped himself to the coin so religiously placed inside the milk-delivery cupboard each night.

"Did Evan have a big truck for the milk?"

"When we first moved to Regina, we lived in a special subdivision for soldiers, called Normandy Heights. The houses were called PMQs, short for private married quarters. On Saturdays, we loved running alongside the truck yakking with Evan through the open doors. There was no seat like in normal vehicles. Evan drove the van standing up like a chariot driver. Down one side of the street and up the other, in rain, snow, and muddy ruts, Evan delivered our milk."

"How did milk stay cold?"

"Well, we had an icebox."

"Where'd you get the ice?"

"From the ice wagon of course, silly."

"Ice wagons in the streets?" Nik's voice rose in surprise.

"Oh, it was amazing, Nik. We could hear the harness bells as Bert, the driver, hawed his horses around the corner. Their hooves carved up the mud, sending clods of earth flying in arcs behind the wagon. I must have been about seven when the ice wagons stopped. Losing the ice wagon put a crimp in our Saturday afternoon shenanigans. Mom was glad, though. She didn't like the filthy ice wagons tearing up the road or the horses shitting everywhere."

"Nanny!"

"I won't tell your mom if you don't. Our secret, eh?"

My god we were lucky, I thought, the smell of tang and sweat fading as the image of the ice wagon retreated.

"It must have been fun growing up in Saskatchewan."

"It was — mosquitoes, thunderstorms, and blizzards aside. I love sharing those times with you."

"And I like hearing the stories."

"I think I was about twelve, just your age, when door-to-door milk delivery stopped. After the war, families wanted new and amazing inventions: margarine packets, plastic packaging, grocery stores where milk was cheaper, and electric refrigerators and stoves. The snub-nosed dairy trucks were relegated to the junkyard."

"That's sad, Nanny. So, plastic's been around that long?"

"Yes. In ten years, we went from iceboxes to electric refrigerators, brown bags to plastic. And now you understand why no one threw the milk caps away. They might have been small, but they were valuable."

"Like my Pokémon collection?"

"Just like it. We always collect and save the things we value," I said.

I pulled him close. The rain continued to fall beyond the window, draping the yard in grey, but inside, Nik's face glowed vibrant. I felt confident that the torch of respect for the past would always burn bright, guiding his steps.

Second Place — **Nonfiction**

Melancholy is close, but not quite right. A better word, perhaps, is bittersweet. "A tendency," writes Susan Cain, "to states of longing, poignancy, and sorrow; an acute awareness of passing time; and a curiously piercing joy at the beauty of the world." This piece starts with a hymn to rain, segues to sacred memorabilia, and then invites the reader to sit in the storytelling chair. In "Rainy Day Treasures," we are then privy to a conversation between grandmother and inquisitive grandson which, through seemingly simple dialogue, solidifies our reasons for living. It isn't about adrenaline-fuelled fantasies or crossing items off a bucket list. Life is about the little moments. Moments of beauty and wonder and magic. And chocolate milk.

— Chris Brauer

Authors and **Judges**

Angie Abdou has published seven books and co-edited *Writing the Body in Motion* and *Not Hockey*, collections of critical essays on Canadian sport literature. Her first novel *The Bone Cage* was a Canada Reads finalist. Her two memoirs hit the Canadian bestseller list. *Booklist* declared *Home Ice: Reflections of a Reluctant Hockey Mom* a "first rate memoir" and a "must-read for parents with youngsters who play organized sports." *Chatelaine Magazine* named her most recent novel, *In Case I Go*, one of the year's most riveting mysteries.

Abdou is a Professor of Creative Writing at Athabasca University.

Charlotte Blair was recently rescued by a dog, has always been rescued by writing, and loves the milder days when she can be rescued by the wind slamming her Harley. She has written poetry for decades, but has only recently been sending it out into the world to fend for itself. Charlotte has had her work published in *Blue Unicorn*, *The Road Not Taken*, *A Journal of Formal Poetry*, and *Arboreal*, among other journals. While she most often writes to form, she has been known to break out in free verse now and then. Charlotte belongs to an eclectic writer's group that can be found at https://we4.ca.

Chris Brauer lives in Creston, BC (on the traditional unceded territory of the Yaqan Nuʔkiy). He teaches elementary school and is the author of four books — most recently his two travel memoirs. Brimming with humour, history, and a celebration of the simple pleasures in life, *Frankincense Land: A Canadian Family in the Sultanate of Oman* details three years living on the shores of the Arabian Sea with his young family. With his terrible sense of direction, and his willingness to go where the wind blows, the author stumbles upon a place that feels more like home than home itself in *Lost Between the Stones and the Sea: A Journey of Discovery in Ireland*. Muttering his motto, "How hard can it be?" Chris has wandered aimlessly in some of the more unique corners of the planet. He is currently working on a book detailing his relationship with the natural world — exploring openness and vulnerability, but especially the magic and mystery found in BC's rainforests. You can follow him on social media.

Chris was the nonfiction judge for the 2024 Askew's Word on the Lake Writing Contest.

David Griffin Brown is an award-winning short fiction writer and co-author of *Immersion and Emotion: The Two Pillars of Storytelling*. He holds a BA in anthropology from UVic and an MFA in creative writing from UBC, and his writing has been published in literary magazines such as *The Malahat Review* and *Grain*. In 2022, he was the recipient of a New Artist grant from the Canada Council for the Arts, which was awarded based on a proposal for his manuscript *Sleeping Cutie and the Destruction of Southgate Mall*. David founded Darling Axe Editing (DarlingAxe.com) in 2018, and as part of his Book Broker interview series, he has compiled querying advice from over one hundred literary agents. David lives in Victoria on the traditional territory of the Esquimalt and Songhees Nations.

David was the fiction judge for the 2024 Askew's Word on the Lake Writing Contest.

Sherry Cassells has written novels, novellas, funny serials, peculiar screenplays, a sitcom, a gazillion short stories, and some scary nonfiction. She writes the kinds of stories she longs for and can rarely find, and her stories have been published in magazines, anthologies, journals, and literary presses. In 2022, she was nominated for a Pushcart Prize. She is passionately involved in many make-believe lives, relevant and purposeful lives of substance, and is always thinking of a story, a sentence, that one word that will slip into position just so. She lives in the wilds of Ontario and is most at home on home row where she chases the cursor with guts and hope. She identifies as italic. See her blog at litbit.ca.

Lindsay Curry is a poet, animal welfare advocate, and ardent volunteer who lives in Kamloops, BC. She used to be a lawyer in what seems to be another lifetime. Lindsay has hosted many open mic nights over the years, where she encouraged everyone who wanted to express themselves creatively to share the art they brought into being. Now she hosts writers circles both online and in person to help create community. Lindsay looks forward to Word on the Lake every year, and in 2013 won the Cheezy Write Contest, her first literary win at her favourite festival.

Annie Dearing is the pen name and secret identity of Debra Turner, the past president of the Shuswap Association of Writers. She is a retired campus library coordinator at Okanagan College, where she had many years experience assisting students and faculty with research, writing, editing, and citation. Recently widowed, she has three adult sons and one grandson. Her favorite types of writing are cathartic poetry and journaling. In her spare time, she practices and teaches quilting.

Jack Dowd graduated from London South Bank University with a BA Hons in Creative Writing in 2015. After graduating, he had several short stories published, including one story winning first place in the Metamorphose's Science Fiction Short Story Competition, before he focused on his novel *Empty Nights*, which he self-published in 2018. Jack writes microfiction, flash fiction, short stories, novels, and novellas while occasionally turning his hand to plays and screenplays. Although he writes in most genres, he can generally be found penning thrillers, horrors, and mysteries. Jack has also participated in NaNoWriMo (National Novel Writing Month) seven times and is currently working on his second novel, *The White Wasteland*. In his spare time, Jack can often be found walking around old castles in England or exploring locations of literary significance in London.

Scott Fitzgerald Gray (9th-level layabout, vindictive good) is a writer of fantasy and speculative fiction, a fiction editor, a story editor, and an editor and designer of roleplaying games — all of which means he finally has the job he really wanted when he was sixteen. He shares his life in the Canadian hinterland with a schoolteacher, two itinerant daughters, and a number of animal and spirit companions. More info on him and his work (some of it even occasionally truthful) can be found by reading between the lines at insaneangel.com.

Scott was the editor of the *Askew's Word on the Lake Anthology 2024*.

Matthew Heneghan is a retired Corporal from the Canadian Forces and a former civilian paramedic. After serving his country and community, Matthew turned to writing as a means of processing his experiences and advocating for mental health awareness. His blog and podcast have gained a modest following, offering insights into the life of a veteran and first responder dealing with PTSD. Matthew's unique perspective, informed by his personal journey through trauma and recovery, positions him as a compelling new voice in nonfiction.

Matthew hosts a podcast by the name of *A Medic's Mind* and writes his experiences on his personal blog: <u>www.amedicsmind.com</u>.

Juliet Hill worked as a theatre musician in the UK for twenty years before moving to Madrid where she started to write. She has written a number of short stories, including "Laughing Boy," a prize winner in the *Writer's Forum* magazine competition; "Property is Theft," shortlisted for the Fiction Desk Newcomer Prize 2015; "Parka Billy," published in the *Momaya Press Short Story Review 2020*; "Untroubled Waters," third-prize winner in the Southport Writer's Circle Short Story Competition 2020; and "Mavis Grind," published in the online magazine *Wishbone Words* (2022).

She is the author of "Onassis and Hoxha" and "The Oboe Player," both published in the *Bedford International Short Story Competition Anthology* (2020/2023), and "The Psychiatrist and the Cleaner" and "Truth or Dare," both shortlisted for the Earlyworks Press 2018 Competition anthology.

"For King and Conscience" is Juliet's second short story to be successful in Canada, after "Bring it to the Yard Sale" was published in the Renaissance anthology *Nothing Without Us Too* (2022). Having spent a year in Saskatoon as a child, this is especially welcome.

Kristine Laco is a satirist, memoirist, and novelist living in Toronto, but asks that you don't hold that against her. She is a graduate of the Creative Writing Certificate Programme at the University of Toronto. Kristine spends her days over-editing a memoir and a contemporary women's fiction novel that will never be perfect while keeping her puppy from getting skunked. Her satire has been in *Slackjaw*, *Greener Pastures*, and *Belladonna Comedy* among others. She has published her personal essays and short stories in five anthologies, literary magazines, and online platforms, including *The Huffington Post* and *Scary Mommy*. You can follow her on all the social media channels @kristinelaco or hang out with her at <u>kristinelaco.com</u> to be the first to know when she finally gets up the nerve to query. Her middle finger is her favourite.

Jill Martin began her post-retirement career in 2012 after thirty years in education. To date, her CV lists six books and many speaking engagements at conferences and other venues. Jill is the author of two Sable Island books: *Return to Sable* (2015); and a year later, *Sable Island in Black and White*, a pictorial book of life on Sable Island at the turn of the twentieth century (Nimbus 2016), which won the 2017 Atlantic Book Democracy award for nonfiction. *From Thistles to Cowpies* (Crossfield 2021) traces the journey of early-twentieth century homesteaders from Sable Island and the Highlands of Scotland to Saskatchewan. Her latest book, *My Life Bridge by Bridge* (Crossfield 2023), is a memoir that takes the reader on a journey into the debilitating power of phobias. From the Greek for "bridge," gephyrophobia affects hundreds of unwilling victims worldwide. Over the past two years, Jill has submitted countless short stories and screenplays to contests. "Always be a work in progress."

Twitter <u>@jillmar23</u>; Facebook <u>Jill Martin Bouteillier Writes</u>; <u>www.key2keyconsulting.ca</u>

Pamela Medland is grateful to live in Nanaimo, the traditional lands of the Snuneymuxw people. Medland's poems have been published in numerous literary journals and anthologies. Her chapbook *Bright Blade* was published in 2020. A full-length poetry collection, *Echo of Ash*, was released in 2021. Medland's poem "Dust" was a winner in the 2020 Askew's Word on the Lake Writing Contest.

Robert J. Sawyer, a member of both the Order of Canada and the Order of Ontario, is one of only eight writers ever (and the only Canadian) to win all three of the world's top awards for best science-fiction novel of the year: the Hugo Award (which he won in 2003 for *Hominids*), the Nebula Award (which he won in 1996 for *The Terminal Experiment*), and the John W. Campbell Memorial Award (which he won in 2006 for *Mindscan*); he also has twelve additional Hugo Award nominations to his credit (including eight others for best novel). Rob's novel *FlashForward* was the basis for the 2009–2010 ABC TV series of the same name, and he was a scriptwriter for that program. A popular keynote and TEDx speaker, Rob has been interviewed over 380 times on TV, over 450 times on radio, and countless times in print. He lives in Mississauga, Ontario. Visit his million-plus-word website at sfwriter.com.

Sheri-D Wilson, mama of Dada, is an award-winning performer and author of fourteen books, four short films, three plays, and four poetry and music albums. She and her work have received many awards and honours, including the Order of Canada, an honorary Doctor of Letters (*Honoris Causa*) from Kwantlen University, Poet Laureate Emeritus of Calgary, the Stephan G. Stephansson Award for Poetry, and the Women of Vision Award.

A strong advocate for social change and community building, Wilson was the founder/artistic director of Calgary Spoken

Word Society (2003–2024) and the Spoken Word Program at the Banff Centre (2005-2012).

Sheri-D splits her time between Calgary and Vancouver with her dog Willow — where she's as busy as the water-table-controlling Emblem of Canada — completing her three-book, one-story trilogy of speculative poetry, *The Oneironaut*, to be published by Write Bloody North.

www.sheridwilson.com | insta @sheri_d_poet | twitter @SheriDWilson | facebook.com/facethepoet

www.ingramcontent.com/pod-product-compliance
Lightning Source LLC
Chambersburg PA
CBHW032253070726
47590CB00016B/2788